TALES FROM THE PAYS D'OC
Re-edited version with new content

Twenty-two tales of life, love and laughter under the Languedoc skies. What is Matthieu doing up an olive tree? Who stole the Indian prawn? Who rescued two hapless Americans at Armageddon Falls? And what is the terrible secret of Chickengate?

Travel to the south of France, feel the scorch of the sun on your shoulders, smell the dust and the lavender and the ripening grapes and follow the adventures of the Saturday Club and the regulars at *L'Estaminet.*

MURDER IN THE PAYS D'OC

The early evening sun gilds the ancient stone steps as they wind round past the church to the river. Only one thing mars this tranquil scene: the body of Gaspard Petit, as he lies twisted at the bottom of the steps, his neck bent at an impossible angle. His open eyes stare up into the unseeing sky.

A tragic accident? Or could it be murder?

Also by Patricia Feinberg Stoner:

At Home in the Pays d'Oc
Tales from the Pays d'Oc

Verse:

Paw Prints in the Butter
The Little Book of Rude Limericks
Pelicans Can't Read

MURDER

in the Pays d'Oc

AND OTHER TALES

Patricia Feinberg Stoner

TALES FROM THE PAYS D'OC
Published 2018 by Fascom
Re-published, with additional material, by Fascom 2022
© Patricia Feinberg Stoner 2018 and 2022

MURDER IN THE PAYS D'OC AND OTHER TALES
Published 2022 by Fascom
© Patricia Feinberg Stoner 2022

Cover design by Cottagewebs
https://www.cottagewebs.co.uk/

Cover image by Bob Stokes
www.bobstokes.co.uk

ISBN 978-1-7397379-1-7

For Purdey (aka Visitor)

whose unexpected arrival started the ball rolling

For Maisie wo keeps us on our toes

And for Himself for his unfailing support

and occasional plotlines

TALES FROM

THE PAYS D'OC

Contents

1. The Saturday Club

Tiger Walk
The Saturday Club
The Man Who Went Four by Fourth
Armageddon Falls
The Rumour Mill
Oops!
The News of the Day
Le Boute-en-train
The Rumour Mill Turns Again

2. Morbignan Tales

Of Vines and Wines and the Prospect of Babies
A Dog Called Useless
Cheeky
An Honorary Good Ol' Boy
Visitor
Chickengate
The Boy in the Water
Boar Wars
The Poet the Thief and the Indian Prawn
Fire! Fire!
Tabac or Not *Tabac*
Blackie
Beginnings

Afterword: From the collected works of Richard Patterson

Who's Who
and Where's Where

Tales from the Pays d'Oc takes place in and around the small market town of St Rémy les Cévennes and the village of Morbignan la Crèbe in the Languedoc, a wine growing region of southern France.

The informal, multi-national gathering known as the Saturday Club takes place in *L'Ane des Cévennes*, a popular café in St Rémy.

Jim	English restaurant owner in Morbignan
Mélodie	his French girl friend
Alice	his sister
Horst	a German construction engineer
Trudi	his wife
Karl Anderssen	Swedish retired linguistics professor
Jeannette	summer visitor to Morbignan, daughter of Gaston Bergerac
Henry	her husband, an Englishman
Useless (Artemis)	their dog
Inez	an exuberant Spanish woman
Gui	her much older, wealthy French husband
Simon	English resident of Morbignan
Zizi	his Parisienne wife
Jean François	owner of *L'Ane des Cévennes*
Mirjam	a retired Dutch head teacher
Elinore	an American
Max	her husband
Blackie	their adopted rabbit
Louis	a local farmer
Adam	an elderly *vigneron*
Gabrielle	his wife of 50 years
Marie Claire	owner of *L'Estaminet* in Morbignan
Gaston Bergerac	a retired *vigneron*
Maître	his dog

Kiki (Cheeky)	local Morbignan bad boy,
Sylvestre	a woodsman
Paulette	his wife
Richard Patterson	a poet
Martha	his wife
Banjax and Bandicoot	their cats
Visitor	their dog
Gaspard Petit	the most hated man in the village
Heloise Dubosc	Gaspard Petit's neighbour
Maurice	her husband
Francois Peitavy	retired *notaire* in Morbignan
Thierry	a *vigneron*
Bernard Durand	a retired policeman
Lili	his wife, a famous singer
The boy in the water	the boy in the water
Matthieu	a plumber
Josette	his wife
Richard (P'tit Mat)	their son
Milou	Matthieu's dog
'Jules et Jim'	two elderly goat farmers
'Papa' Pardieu	mayor of Morbignan la Crèbe
Joséphine	his secretary
Davide	former mayor of Morbignan
Madame Brieux	the cat lady

Three little words...

Bisou	A kiss. The traditional Languedocian salutation is three kisses on the cheeks: left, right, left
Un demi	a half litre of beer
Vigneron	a producer of wine

PART ONE

THE SATURDAY CLUB

Tiger Walk

Five o'clock on a July Saturday. The tiger prowled the waking market of St Rémy des Cévennes.

The sun, just rising, cast a grey aura over the path along which he stalked. His tail twitched as the glories of the night's hunt ghosted his consciousness. Eldritch cries split the air above his head.

'Salut, Jean Pierre!'

'Salut! ça va?'

'Quelle belle journée.'

To the tiger they were as the calls of distant birds, and he paid them no mind.

Along the path loomed huge shapes, spilling unidentifiable odours. To the tiger they were as the boulders of the seashore, and he paid them no mind.

Something landed – thunk! – on the path before him, startling him so that he reared back, stiff-legged, the fur bristling on his arched spine. Cautiously he sniffed – here was food! With a ravenous snatch he gulped it down; its origin was unknown to him but he paid it no mind.

The tiger prowled on.

Nine o'clock.

The sun, not yet cruel, cast a friendly glow over the market.

It lit up the old woman with her worn wicker basket, examining cherries, squeezing peaches, sniffing out bargains on the fruit stall.

It illuminated the goat's cheese man, his skimpy beard waggling as he bleated his wares: *'Chèvre frais, chèvre frais!'*

It gilded the substantial form of the German woman, turning over the tawdry blouses on the *friperie*.

It peeped slyly over the awning outside the *Café de l'Ane*, where the summer residents were beginning to gather.

The tiger prowled on.

Ten o'clock.

At number 4 *Rue de l'Eglise*, Mme Dujardin was calling her pet. '*Minou, minou, minou*!' She rattled the bag of dry biscuit, coaxing. There was no response.

Next door at number three, replete with chicken, the tiger raised his head from his snug nest of pillows. He heard Mme Dujardin's anxious cries: to the tiger they were as the chattering of monkeys in the treetops high above him, and he paid them no mind.

'Good cat,' said Mrs Dickinson fondly, stroking his ears. 'Good cat.'

The Saturday Club

St Rémy les Cévennes. Medieval town, market town, birthplace – or so they say – of a famous composer. Twenty-five kilometres from the Mediterranean coast, beneath the Cévennes mountains, nestled amid the vines and the olives and the sunflowers, baking under the summer sun of the Languedoc.

The long central avenue of St Rémy les Cevennes, *La rue du quatorze juillet*, slopes steeply upwards from south to north. It is here that the Saturday market has its home. Start at the bottom and delight in the rich aromas of fruit and vegetables laid out for your temptation. Wander up through the racks of gaudy clothing: flimsy skirts and see-through tops, bright T shirts with sporting or cheeky slogans, cheap and cheerful shoes in the latest fashions. They won't last long, but next year you can be trendy all over again. Emerge at the top of the market and you'll find the goat-cheese man and the stalls of aromatic *saucisson* and glistening olives set out in half-barrels for you to dip into.

Tucked behind the *friperie* – pre-loved clothing from Paris at ridiculously low prices – and the purveyor of *nems*, irresistible Vietnamese delicacies, you'll find *Le Café de l'Ane*. It is named in honour of Robert Louis Stevenson, who famously walked through the Cévennes mountains from Le Monastier to Saint Jean du Gard, accompanied by his faithful donkey Modestine.

It is here that the Saturday Club assembles. In winter it is a meagre affair: the few remaining residents, those who haven't returned to busy lives in Paris or Lille, London or Manchester, huddle over their coffees and *demis* and bemoan the weather. For the weather in this part of the Languedoc, like the weather in every part of the world, is not what it used to be. Bright, crisp winters with the occasional freezing snap are a thing of the past. Now the rain slants in on a spiteful wind and the houses, with their thick stone walls and flagged floors, are nowhere near as welcoming as they were in the hot and glorious days of July and August.

But in summer the Saturday club is resplendent - indeed, St Rémy itself is resplendent: its population doubled and trebled by the in-swelling tide of holidaymakers and seasonal visitors from the north of France and the north of Europe. The market is a Babel of accents: German and Spanish, English and Dutch, even a few French voices make themselves heard.

And here they come, on a sweltering July Saturday as the town prepares for the festivities of Bastille Day. Here the sophisticates of St Rémy meet their country cousins, from Morbignan and Les Herbes, Les Schistes and Sainte-Marie-du-Vent.

Jim and Alice, as usual, are the first to arrive at the café. A pair of middle-aged expats, brother and sister, they have come to roost in the nearby village of Morbignan la Crèbe.

Jim and his French girlfriend Mélodie run a restaurant on the hill above Morbignan. Famous for its warm welcome and uncertain menu, *La Truite Dorée* is a magnet for every local or itinerant musician - for Jim, although no musician himself, is passionate about jazz.

Alice's 'apartment' is a jumble of rooms attached to Jim and Mélodie's rambling stone-built farmhouse. She is rarely there.

The pair settle into the choicest table on the shady terrace; the café owner, unbidden, bustles over to greet them with a glass of iced Perrier and a small black coffee. It is, after all, only ten o'clock: the serious drinking won't begin for at least half an hour.

Horst and Karl soon make an appearance, deep in conversation as usual. They make an incongruous couple – Karl tall, brisk, Nordic, and the little round Horst with his shining pate and schoolmasterly glasses. Trudi, Horst's cool, blonde wife, will not join them for an hour or more. Karl is listening to yet another of Horst's preposterous money-making schemes, nodding sagely; or could it be that they are discussing menus: the virtues of basil versus mint in a tomato salad, the wisdom of ras-al-hanout in a tabbouleh? Both men are passionate foodies.

There is a flurry of grey and white fur, a cacophony of excited yelps as Useless hurls herself at the group, tail wagging and tongue lolling. Towed in her wake is Jeannette, laughing breathlessly and apologising to everyone. Her husband, Henry Prendergast – universally known as *l'anglais* - brings up the rear.

'Hello, Jeannette!' Jim has a glint in his eye. 'I didn't know you were here. You're early, aren't you? You usually come in September. Oh, good morning Henry, I didn't see you there,' he adds hastily.

Henry is having a hard time keeping a straight face. He's well aware that Jim has, shall we say, warm feelings towards Jeannette, and that most of the men in the group are convinced she could have done better in the husband department. He manages to hold it together, though. After all, he has a reputation to live up to: *l'anglais*, the pompous Englishman complete with pin stripes, bowler and furled umbrella. In reality, he possesses none of these things. Later, alone, he and Jeannette will have a giggle about it.

'*Bonjour tout le monde*,' says Henry carefully, taking care with his pronunciation. 'What is everyone having?'

It's a rhetorical question: Jim, Horst and Karl will each have a *demi,* a half-litre, of the local beer, Alice can be coaxed into ordering a *petit blanc*. It is Saturday, after all.

Inez and Gui are squabbling as they arrive at the table with Simon and Zizi.

'Just ten minutes, *querido*! Look at Zizi's shoes, they are *mono,* no, very cute? I just want to go and see this little boutique on the *rue d'arcy.* Just to look…'

'Just to spend my money, *hein*? Haven't you got enough shoes, Inez?'

'Oh go on, Gui, let her have her fun. You can afford it,' Simon butts in with his usual tact. Zizi rolls her eyes but says nothing.

'Oh well, OK, but strictly ten minutes, *chérie*. I shall be keeping an eye on the time.' Twenty-two carat gold cufflinks catch the sun as Gui ostentatiously consults his Patek Philippe.

Inez flounces off on six-inch stilettos; the remaining three find chairs and join the group.

'No Mirjam today?' says Simon. 'That's odd. She's usually so desperate not to miss anything that she's the first one here. Oh!' He jumps: something warn and wet has connected with his bare knee.

'Oh, it's you. Hello Useless.' Simon bends to ruffle the dog's ears. 'Honestly, Jeannette, haven't you found a name for her yet?' Simon continues. 'You can't expect the poor girl to go through life with a name like Useless.'

'She's got a name,' Henry is quick to explain. 'Her kennel name is *Silverleaf Daddy's Delight*.' He pauses to let the explosion of laughter die down, then:

'See? And anyway, Useless suits her.'

Jean-François arrives to take their orders, putting an end to further debate. As they sip their drinks, Mirjam explodes into the café. Her face is red, her usually immaculate hair is standing on end and she is breathless with excitement.

'You'll never believe what I've just seen...' she begins.

The group settle back with a collective sigh of contentment. The day's gossip-fest has begun.

The Man Who Went Four by Fourth

Karl Anderssen was a Swede. Everybody knew he was a Swede. He *looked* Swedish, dammit, standing well over six feet tall, with his broad shoulders and his jaunty red-blond beard and his ice-keen blue eyes. Self-styled retired linguistics professor from Malmö, that was Karl.

You greeted him with a firm handshake – woe betide man or woman who tried the sloppy Southern *bisou* (kiss) on him – and minded your manners while he was about.

Mirjam, mind you, had her suspicions, but then Mirjam would. A little surreptitious digging revealed a short and somewhat inglorious career in Malmö as an assistant lecturer. True, his mother was Swedish, but his *Papa,* though of Swedish descent, was born and bred in Montpellier, as was Karl himself.

And was the community of St Rémy shocked by this deception? Did it rise to a man and woman and cast out the impostor? It did not.

After all, he was a genial sort of chap, always quick to stand his round at the café and often to be seen, of a market day in St Remy, at or at least near the table of the Saturday club.

In honour of the occasion, he would change into his best jeans – hardly torn at all - and, depending on the weather, a checked woollen shirt or a rather tattered T-shirt emblazoned with the words "Sochi 2014".

One other thing that everybody knew about Karl Anderssen was that he was a confirmed bachelor. No, not in the nudge-nudge wink-wink sort of way: there were no pretty little boys tucked away in his past, or in the corners of his rather gloomy three-story *Maison de Maître* on the *Rue Vermier*

No, it was just that Karl Anderssen did not marry. Had not married. Would never marry. Rumour had it that there had been a terrible tragedy: She Loved Another or She Died Tragically Young or some such; but rumour will ever have it thus.

Now this is not to say that Anderssen was without passion. Far from it: what Karl was passionate about was, or rather were, four-by-fours. Any big, butch vehicle with large knobbly tyres and an excess of mud flaps would set his eyes a-spark, but what he really loved were Land

Rovers. And by Land Rovers, of course, he meant Series and Defenders. Not for him the high-falutin' Range Rover, nor the serviceable but still sleek Discovery – these he called Bland Rovers, and he treated them with disdain.

It started... well it actually started when he was five years old. One evening in the café, after perhaps one more *pastis* than was wise, he confided the tale. '*Mamma* and I were in the big toy store in Montpellier, we were looking for a birthday present for my sister. I saw a little orange car, about the size of that cigarette packet of yours, Horst, and I *really* wanted it. I didn't know this, of course, but it was a scale model of a Land Rover Series 1.

'*Mamma* said no, it was not my birthday, I would have to wait. According to my mother, who was always prone to exaggerate, I lay on the floor and kicked my feet and howled. I am sure this is not true. Nevertheless, she did not buy me the toy that day – very sensibly in my opinion: children should not be spoiled.' Here Karl cast a stern eye at Louisette, whose whining, pestering six-year-old was as usual creating mayhem in the far corner of the café.

'However,' he resumed, 'when my birthday came, there it was, in a box with a ribbon bow on it – the little orange Land Rover. How I loved that car.'

'Not changed much, then, have you, Karl, if that heap in the car park's anything to go by?' Jim was always the first of the group to say what everyone else was thinking.

To be honest, it was a bit of a monstrosity. Karl had acquired a Defender 110 with a camper body on the back and Paris-Dakar Rally stickers on the bumper. He could just see himself driving gloriously into an African sunset, beard flowing in the wind and some Nubian beauty by his side. The fact that holes had rusted through the floor of the cab and the suspension was, as Jim elegantly put it, 'dragging its arse along the ground' was no deterrent.

'Perhaps you should enter the *concours*,' Horst put in, tongue firmly in cheek. He pointed to a poster pinned to the front of the bar. Anderssen peered at it: sure enough, the drivers of St Rémy and beyond were invited, this very Wednesday, to take part in a trial of skill and dexterity on a course designed by the assistant editor of *L'Automobile,* no less. There would be a cash prize for the winner. Anderssen studied the poster carefully. A faraway look came into his eyes.

16

'Yes, perhaps I should…' he mused.

'*Nein*, for heaven's sake, I was joking!' Horst protested. 'It's for little cars, sporty cars, not for great galumphing things like yours.'

Karl raised an eyebrow and buried himself in his *demi*. The conversation was closed.

The event was to be held on a piece of ground called the football field, on the outskirts of St Rémy. Perhaps it had once indeed been a sports ground, but its hard-won green had long since desiccated into a stony desert. Its few remaining benches were greyed and splintery and listed perilously under the relentless sun. A lone fig tree, which had grown weed-like through the weeds, offered a scant shade which the first-comers were quick to claim.

On the course, the officials scurried about like yellow beetles, sweating in their Panamas and high-viz vests. Clipboards tucked importantly beneath their arms, they blew shrill whistles and waved a motley assortment of flags. With a cheerful Gallic disregard for the regulations, they lined up the contestants on a first-come, first-served basis.

There was a substantial turnout of Saturday Club members. Horst and Trudi were there, as were Jim and Mélodie, with Alice in tow. Gui had brought Inez and her sister Pilar. Even Mirjam had deigned to attend. Had they come to support their friend? Or was it, as Jim put it, to see him "make a right prairie 'at of himself"?

They regarded the line-up with some hilarity. First to go was an entry from Morbignan: a nippy little red Peugeot 205 driven by Kiki from the *tabac*. Behind it came, in order, a Fiat Panda, a Citroën 2cv, a Citroën Diane, Karl in his bungalow-sized Land Rover, another Fiat Panda and a beach buggy.

The course was tight: winding between stacks of tyres, with a wicked-looking chicane just before the finish.

'Looks like it's a toss-up between Karl and the beach buggy for last place,' Gui remarked. 'It's a sure bet one of them will break down halfway round.'

'Don't dismiss the beach buggy,' said Mirjam, who made a point of knowing everything there was to know. 'That's Louis' car, and it's got an Alfa Romeo engine. Goes like…'

17

'Like shit off a shovel?' Jim supplied helpfully. Mirjam tutted and examined her fingernails.

From his lofty seat in the Defender's cab, Karl too was surveying the opposition. The Peugeot did a flawless round, deftly negotiating the third and tightest bend with just a tap of foot on brake, bravely accelerating through the chicane and finishing with a flourish, spinning the car in a full handbrake turn. His time went up on the ramshackle notice board that served as a score sheet: two minutes twenty-eight seconds.

Karl pondered the odds. Manoeuvring the Land Rover through the tight turns was an impossibility, but there was a way... When the marshal's flag went down, he took off like a bat out of hell, skidding the unwieldy vehicle round the piled-up tyres, skirting disaster by a whisker. The final turn was fiendish. Taking a deep breath, Karl stamped on the accelerator and drove straight for the obstacle. A collective gasp went up from the onlookers as he barrelled through, sending tyres flying in all directions. A canny – or fortunate – snapper from *Midi Libre* clicked his shutter at the crucial moment, earning himself a front-page by-line and hero status for a week.

The *concours* officials scratched their heads. Had Dr Anderssen cheated? He had only touched one obstacle – correction: he had obliterated it – yet by this very strategy he had shaved several seconds off his time. As they debated the rights and wrongs of the matter, the decision was taken out of their hands. A tortured screech of metal on metal assaulted their ears.

The Land Rover halted in its triumphal charge towards the finishing line. Karl jumped out and prostrated himself beneath the vehicle. The crowd held its breath. Had the chassis collapsed? Had all the wheel bearings fallen out? There was no obvious sign of damage. Half a dozen locals rushed across – whether to help or to jeer was debatable. Karl peeled himself off the ground and gingerly inserted himself back into the driver's seat. He set off at a walking pace. *Screech!* He slammed his foot on the brake. Silence. He set off again, more slowly this time. *Screech!*

There was nothing for it. Slowly, he limped off the course, pursued by the shrieks of the damned. The marshals instantly awarded him the wooden spoon.

In the café that night, however, Karl Anderssen entered to a standing round of applause. The Saturday Club hadn't had so much fun since the time Gui got locked in the café overnight and emerged drunk as a skunk and waving his trousers above his head.

'How's the Landy?' Horst wanted to know. 'Can it be fixed? Did you find out what the problem was?'

Karl winked. Solemnly, he drew from his pocket a small envelope. Carefully laying it on the table, he withdrew from its depths a small stone. A very small stone: no more than a speck of gravel.

'*Ecce lapidus*' he said portentously. 'Behold the stone. It must have been thrown up when I went through the tyres. It had lodged itself between the brake and the brake pad; I removed it when I got home.'

'Well, I hope you've learned your lesson,' said Mirjam. 'That monster of yours had no place in a little *concours* like that, now did it?'

'Perhaps not,' said Karl, 'but it was fun.'

The offending stone was ceremoniously taped to a scrap of paper and framed: it hangs above the bar in *L'Estaminet* to this day, *Ecce Lapidus* inscribed in a flowing freehand beneath it.

Armageddon Falls

'Kumquats,' she says loudly and distinctly. 'KUM-quats, *oui*?'

Madame Duval, on the fruit stall, exchanges an eye roll with her neighbour the cheesemonger. The stout American lady is getting agitated; who knows what she wants?

The *fruitière* shrugs. Thierry Malmaison completes the sale of *un demi-salé* to a regular customer and turns to watch the fun.

Elinore is close to tears: the day is going all wrong. It had seemed like such a fun idea to go round this darling little market and pick up ingredients for their Saturday night dinner. Max would expect something special. But the fluent French she had acquired at her expensive school in Boston was met with blank stares here. Were these people retarded?

Eight inches shorter but just as wide, Alice popped up by her elbow.

'You won't get kumquats here, ducks. Wrong country, wrong season.'

Elinore gaped at her. She had seen this fussy little person several times back in Morbignan, but she was always gabbling away in French. To hear her speaking English like a native was a shock. Elinore was not to know that Alice's French was scarcely better than her own, albeit delivered with more aplomb.

Alice, in turn, was considering Elinore and debating an important question. Should she take pity on the American and invite her to join the Saturday Club table at *L'Ane des Cévennes*? She knew what Jim would say.

'That phoney? Calls herself an artist, then moans that there's nothing to paint here except olive trees and sunflowers. Well, it was good enough for old Vincent, and she ain't no Van Gogh.'

Like many expats, Jim had decided to be more French than the French – or, to be precise, more Occitan than his Languedoc neighbours. The landscape, the sun, the weather-beaten faces, the silver grey of the olives and the silver green of the vines – all these were his, now; he took it as a personal affront that anyone should fail to appreciate them as he did.

Alice was made of kinder stuff.

'Why don't you come and have a drink with us?' she soothed. 'There's a whole bunch of us meet on a Saturday: French and German and Dutch and even a few Americans.'

Elinore hesitated. Max had "suggested" that they meet at 12:30 sharp at the *Café des Artistes*. He did not like having his plans interfered with. A worm of rebellion turned in Elinore's not-unremarkable breast.

'Why, yes, that would be neat,' she enthused. She took out her Samsung Galaxy; to her chagrin, Alice seemed unaware that it was the latest model.

'Max? Change of plan. We're meeting at the café at the top end of the market. It's called *L'Ane des Cévennes*. See you there.'

She hadn't paused for breath. Max always let his phone go to voicemail; he would get the message when he got it, she thought with a small spark of glee.

Walking back up the market street, Elinore gazed about her. It was so colourful, so quaint: those old women with their wrinkled faces and straw baskets - why, they were right out of a movie.

It was the first weekend in July and the Saturday Club was at its height. Seven faces turned and scrutinised Elinore, who felt an unaccustomed shyness at approaching the table. Alice, though, was in her element: commandeering two chairs from a nearby table, chivvying the group to budge up and make room, ostentatiously exchanging *bisous* with the café owner when he came up to take their order.

Elinore just knew her face was shining and her hair escaping from the wispy bun on top of her head. Murmuring an excuse, she turned in search of a ladies' room.

'*C'est par là, Madame,*' said Jean-François kindly, and pointed her in the right direction. As she approached the *toilettes*, Elinore was startled to see a smartly dressed elderly gentleman emerge from the single stall, still checking the zip on his cream trousers. Really, this country was so... *European*.

At the table, the Saturday Club was in full inquisitive spate.

'They're sort of neighbours of ours in Morbignan,' Alice was explaining importantly. 'They are renting Jean Legros' house, next door to the Pattersons. They come from Michigan, he's an electronics engineer, I think, and she's an artist.'

'*Calls* herself an artist,' interrupted Jim.

Alice ignored him. 'Anyway, the poor thing was down at the fruit stall, the one opposite the café with the bamboo chairs. She was trying to buy kumquats, of all things...'

Elinore was back in their midst.

'They're for a special dessert I make. I don't know what's so odd about kumquats: they always have them in the mall back home.'

No-one wanted to know about the special dessert.

'Done much painting lately?' enquired Jim innocently.

'Elinore pouted. 'Yeah, I been painting, but honestly when you've seen one vine you've seen them all.'

This remark was met with a blank silence. Hurrying to be tactful, Inez cut in:

'And what else have you been doing since you've been here? Have you seen any of the sights?'

Fortunately for Elinore, who was opening her mouth to say, 'What sights?' Max chose that moment to appear.

'Lenny, I told you to meet me at *Le Café des Artistes*. Why the change of plan?'

'Why not? And don't call me Lenny. Alice was kind enough to invite me to meet some of her friends. I thought you might like a change.'

Elinore knew very well that there was nothing Max liked less than a change of plan, and the look he gave her confirmed it. She returned the look with a wifely smile.

Jim decided to rescue the situation. Beer, he knew, was the great leveller.

'Hello, old man,' he said, holding out a rather grubby paw. 'I'm Jim, Alice's brother, and you must be Max. Can I buy you a *demi*?'

Max eyed him coldly.

'Thank you, no. I would prefer a small scotch.' He turned and snapped his fingers in the direction of Jean François. The silence at the table was glacial.

'Now, dear, that's not the way we do things here,' Elinore said quickly. 'Now sit down and behave.'

Max subsided, but there was a quiver in his moustache that Elinore recognised all too well.

'What shall we do tomorrow?' she asked brightly.

'Why should we do anything?' Max was not to be mollified.

'Well, it's your day off. I thought you might like to go out and do something.'

'Like what?'

A babble of suggestions greeted this question.

'Have you been to Montpellier?' asked Mirjam. 'It's quite lovely, and it has a very old medical school. The oldest in the world, I believe.'

'I *work* in Montpellier for gawdsakes,' said Max. 'In a hospital. Why would I want to go and see some crummy old medical school on my day off?'

Mirjam turned her back and began an animated conversation with Trudi.

'What about the Pont Nic?' suggested Jim.

'What's that?' Elinore asked. Max was still glowering.

'*Le Pont du Vieux Nicolas,*' Horst put in. 'It is a spectacular bridge over a gorge through which runs the Hérault river. There is a swimming place on the river and a café. It will also be possible if you wish to rent a kayak or canoe to go down the river.'

'A kayak?' that sounds like fun. Max fancied himself a sportsman.

Sunday morning dawned promising to be what Elinore privately called HBG – hot, blue and gold. She selected her shadiest sun hat and a straw panama for Max, and packed a cooler full of cheese, olives, tomatoes and wine with a fresh *baguette* from the *boulangerie* on the corner.

Max had spent half an hour with his Garmin the evening before, plotting out the exact route, the journey's duration, the elevation, the mileage and the probable fuel consumption.

They were on the road by eight. Elinore would have liked a lie-in, but 'It'll take over an hour to get there,' said her husband. 'If we are there much later than nine I doubt if we'll find a parking space.'

Maddeningly, he was right. As they drove down the stony track the car park outside the café was filling up fast.

'Shall we stop for a drink first?' said Elinore hopefully, eyeing the little wooden shack with its tables and chairs set out under colourful umbrellas. A glass of something cool overlooking the spectacular gorge was very tempting.

'Not if you want to get a decent picnic spot and some shade,' said Max. 'Come along Lenny, let's go and stake our claim.'

Max shouldered the cool bag and beach chairs and set off briskly. Eyeing the steep path down to the river, Elinore was rummaging in her bag for espadrilles, but her husband shouted,

'Come on, come on, don't dawdle!' So, laden with beach umbrella, swim bag, towels and a kilo of cherries bought by the roadside, Elinore slip-slid down the slope in her strappy wedge-heeled sandals.

By the time she reached the spot deemed suitable by Max, he had already unfolded one beach chair and dived into the cooler; he was sitting at his ease with a glass of chilled rosé in his hand.

'What kept you?' he said.

Muttering something which might have been an endearment, but probably wasn't, Elinore set about making herself comfortable.

The sun was hot and making her drowsy.

'Shall we have a paddle?' she asked after a while.

'You can if you want to. I'm fine where I am.'

Elinore slipped off her sandals and dipped a toe in the water.

'It's freezing!' she gasped.

'You were the one who wanted to paddle,' retorted Max.

Ignoring him, Elinore waded further into the river, enjoying the feel of smooth stones beneath her feet, the swirl and pop of the water round her ankles. She tipped her head back and let the fierce sun play on her face for just a few delicious moments before her wiser self whispered "sun block" and sent her scurrying back to their shady spot.

After they had eaten the picnic that Elinore set out, and after she had cleared it away, Max was fidgeting.

'Now, how about those kayaks?' he exclaimed, bouncing on his toes.

'Can't we have a few moments' rest first?' said Elinore plaintively. She knew she was fighting a losing battle.

'Oh, come *on*, Lenny. Don't be a spoilsport. Let's go get us a kayak and have a paddle down this river you seem so fond of.'

Sighing, Elinore got up.

'All right, but you'll have to take all this stuff back to the car. I'm not climbing up there and back down again in this heat.'

The man at the kayak rental place eyed them with wary concern. '*Vouz avez déja fait du kayaking?*' he asked them. Then, seeing their blank faces, 'You have done zees before?'

'How hard can it be?' Max wanted to know. 'Just get the damn boat into the water and we'll be fine. It's only a little river, for gawdsakes.'

24

The kayak looked awfully small for two not insubstantial people. Elinore regarded it fearfully. 'Are you sure we'll be all right in that?' she asked.

'We'll be just fine,' Max repeated. He stepped into the little bright yellow boat, which rocked alarmingly, and settled himself on one of the two benches, leaving the boat man to help Elinore in. The man handed each of them a paddle and with a strong push sent the little craft out into the middle of the river.

'*Bonne chance!*' he called after them, and Elinore wondered if she detected sarcasm in his voice.

For a few minutes Elinore said nothing, concentrating on steering in a straight line. Max dug his paddle deep into the water and her gentler dips were scarcely enough to keep them from veering off into the left bank. When at last she raised her head, she almost gasped at the beauty of it. The river slid between steep rocky walls studded with gorse and scrub; the sky was a deeper blue than she had ever seen.

Max had stopped talking. Elinore closed her eyes and surrendered to the noises that silence makes: the plash and gurgle of their oars meeting the water, the busy scratch of the crickets, the occasional chatter of a pair of quarrelsome magpies.

Their peace was shattered as they negotiated a leisurely bend. A group of boys were playing at the water's edge, smirking twelve-to-thirteen-year-olds with uncertain voices and a sneer in their eyes. They greeted the new arrivals with jeers and whistles. Three of the lads had kayaks of their own, steering them expertly through the water as though the boats were an extension of their own bodies. They swooped and glided through the shallows, their grace mocking the heavy-handed foreigners in their rented craft.

Max stared straight ahead, refusing to acknowledge the boys; Elinore attempted a wave and a timid smile. Suddenly one of the older boys manoeuvred alongside them. Bare-chested, he wore only cut-off jeans and his pre-adolescent body was a deep mahogany brown.

Brushing back a tangle of chestnut curls he called across to them: '*Attention! 'Ya un barrage en bas*! Be careful.'

'What's he saying?' asked Elinore anxiously. 'Why do we have to be careful?'

'Ignore him. He's just a smart-ass. Trying to get a rise out of us.'

25

The water seemed to be getting shallower; Elinore could see the glint of sun on the pebbles beneath them. 'No, he really was trying to tell us something,' she insisted. 'Max, I think we better turn back.'

'Nonsense,' said her husband. 'I'm enjoying this and I'm darned if I'm going to let some snotty little French punk spoil it for me.'

At that point, there was a gentle bump and they ran out of river.

'Dam!' said Elinore.

Max looked startled; even this mild expletive was unusual for his wife.

'Yes: dam' said Elinore, who had been searching a mental dictionary. 'Or weir. That's what *barrage* means. That's what those boys were trying to warn us about.

Sure enough, the kayak was going nowhere. It was firmly stuck on the riverbed while the water went on its way, chuckling as it splashed down a dizzying drop of at least eight inches before gathering itself into a deep pool below.

'What now?' they spoke simultaneously.

'Well,' said Elinore, I suggest you get out and push.'

Max glanced down at his Gucci sandals. 'I'm not getting into the water,' he said flatly.

'Well, I'm certainly not,' she retorted, as she settled her backside more comfortably on the bench.

Shouts, laughter and whoops of glee erupted from round the bend, followed by the three boys in their kayaks, skimming the water like dragonflies. The boy who had spoken to them, clearly the leader of the little gang, slalomed to a stop beside the stranded Americans. His lighter craft – and his lighter weight – kept him afloat above the riverbed.

'You have the problem?' His eyes teased them.

'Yes, we're stuck,' said Elinore, quite unnecessarily in Max's opinion.

With a word to his companions, the boy scrambled out of his kayak. Producing a coil of rope, he attached it to their boat's mooring ring. All three boys took up the slack and heaved; in seconds they were floating free. Without more ado, the lads grabbed the kayak, turned it round and with a firm push sent it back the way it had come.

'Paddle, Max, paddle!' hissed Elinore, grabbing her own blade. As they got under way, she looked back at the three grinning youngsters. 'Thank you!' she called. '*Merci*!'

'*Avec plaisir,*' the boy shouted back. 'Anything for our Eeenglish cousins.' He stood up straight and saluted crisply. 'God save the Queen,' he shouted.

Elinore didn't need to look. She knew Max's face was turning purple.

The Rumour Mill

The Bastille Day fireworks were over and done; the season was officially open. As usual, the Saturday market in St Rémy was heaving; snatches of conversation in English, German, Dutch, Russian and the twanging tones of America fought with the cries of the vendors.

At the bottom end of the market, the fruit stalls spilled a cornucopia of melons and strawberries, cherries and peaches, their scents voluptuous and enticing in the heat. Further up, the goat-farmer from *Les Chevrettes* was eyeing up plump Marie-Claude as she presided over the olives, green and golden, black and luscious, redolent of smoky bars and midnight song.

On the *friperie* stall, thick-fingered Frau Eberhardt lifted a skimpy top to her breasts and studied her reflection, turning this way and that in the clouded mirror. Hidden behind their hands, Josiane and Marie, employees for a day, giggled teenage derision.

Red-faced beneath his panama, Jim battled his way up the steep cobbled street, negotiating a path through shopping trolleys, small children and excitable dogs. *Le Café de l'Ane* was crowded, but he knew that Alice, savvy with the experience of many a St Rémy summer, would have got there early and secured their table in the coolest part of the room.

'Ouf!' he dumped his shopping bag, spilling cherries and asparagus and *fromage de chèvre* over the tiled floor.

'Hot, is it?' Alice smiled innocently up at her brother.

Jim regarded her somewhat balefully. 'Hot? I'll say so. I swear the Saturday market gets worse every July. Grockles everywhere – it took me ten minutes to walk up from the *tabac*.' Jim flourished his hat and adopted a comedic stance. '*I say! I say! I say!* what is the second language of Saint Rémy in the summer?'

With a long-suffering 'All right, I'll go along with it' expression, Alice obliged: 'English?'

'No – French. Boom-boom!'

'*Nein!*' Horst strode into the café in time to hear the punchline. Carefully smoothing his crisp khaki shorts, he sat down beside Alice.

'You are quite wrong,' he told them dead-pan. 'Ze second language here in ze summer is Cherman. Ze French all go to ze mountains. Vot are you trinking?'

Alice dutifully groaned at the self-parody: it would have been rude not to. 'Just for that you can buy me a glass of wine.'

'A *demi* for me, please,' said Jim, 'and as cold as you like.'

Horst waved a manicured finger at Jean-François, the café owner, who bustled up looking harassed but smiling. '*Salut, tout le monde*,' he greeted them. 'Hello Alice – *mmmwah*!' The ritual kiss. '*Bonjour* Horst, *bonjour* Jim.' The ritual handshake.

As Horst was placing his order – 'Two *demis* and a *petit blanc*, please Jean François.' - the delectable Jeannette came sashaying through the crowded café.

'Jeannette! Ho, Jeannette, over here!' cried Horst and Jim in unison.

'No Henry today, then?' leered Jim, edging a little closer.

Jeannette shook her head, bursting with exciting news. 'Hi everyone. No, Henry's had to go back to England for a couple of days. Say, did you hear about the shooting?'

They crowded closer, agog. 'No! What shooting?'

'Last night in *La Cloche d'Or*. Man was shot dead. It's bound to be in the paper.'

'Wait, I've got it here.' Jim delved into his groceries and came up with a crumpled and rather fruit-stained *Midi Libre*. There was an expectant pause as he rattled through the pages, a sigh of disappointment as he shook his head. 'No... nothing in here at all.'

Alice's nose twitched with importance. 'Did you say *La Cloche d'Or*? We heard it!'

Two enthralled pairs of eyes swivelled in her direction. Jim's gaze was altogether more sceptical.

'You heard it? The shooting? Really?' Jeannette was fizzing with curiosity.

'Well, no, not the actual shooting. But you know our house is just around the corner from *La Cloche D'Or*. And there was this awful row at about two o'clock in the morning. I know it was two because I couldn't sleep and I heard the clock strike. I looked out of the window but I couldn't see anything. So that's what it was.'

Inez joined the group in a flurry. '*Hola todos!*   Alice – *mmmwah!* Jim – *mmmwah!* Horst – *mmmwah!* Gui is just parking the car. Ah,

Jean-François, just in time! *Mmmwah! Un pastis et un demi*, please. Ah, Gui! That was quick.'

Gui darted into the café, glancing beadily round the room before trotting to their table. He fanned himself elaborately with a tattered straw hat.

'*Bonjour tous et toutes*. Yes, I found a spot in the *Parking Quatorze*. Say, did you hear about the shooting?'

'I was just about to tell them...' interrupted Inez, but Alice was there first.

'I know. I heard the shot. So, what actually happened?'

'Man shot dead in *La Cloche d'Or* on Thursday, according to Jeannette,' Jim began.

'Oh, no, it wasn't *in La Cloche d'Or*.' This was Inez again. 'It was in *L'Auberge de l'Abbaye*. It was the *owner* of *La Cloche d'Or*. Some kind of drugs scam went wrong.'

They looked at her aghast. Lucien, the *patron* of *La Cloche d'Or*, was friendly, and his restaurant was a great favourite among the ex-pat community.

'Lucien? I really liked him,' squealed Alice. 'I never knew he was into drugs? Is he dead?'

'Yes,' said Inez.

Two days later, Jim was in St Rémy doing a bit of shopping and found Franck, a local artist, in the *boulangerie* twinkling over a box of *patisseries*. Proffering a limp, paint-stained hand, Franck went straight to the topic of the day.

'Did you hear about the shooting?'

'Yes I did. It's awful. Poor Lucien. I really liked him. But I never knew he was a drug dealer.'

Franck looked at him blankly. 'What are you talking about?'

'Lucien, you know, from *La Cloche d'Or*. Got shot in *L'Auberge de l'Abbaye*. Some kind of drugs scam, it seems.'

'No he didn't. I mean it wasn't Lucien. And it was nothing to do with *L'Auberge*. It was in the *tabac* next door to *La Cloche d'Or*.'

'Lucien was shot in the *tabac*?'

Franck was getting impatient. 'No, no, *no!*' he squealed. 'A man held up the *tabac*. Shot *Louis*. Only got away with 50€ and a couple of packs of Gauloises. Lucien saw it all.'

This was sad news. 'Louis got shot? Is he dead?'

'In intensive care. Apparently, his chances are fifty-fifty.'

The following Saturday Jim and Alice were hesitating in the doorway of the café. 'Oh come on, Alice,' coaxed Jim, 'surely we've got time for a coffee. I think we've earned it after all that shopping.'

'A coffee! A beer more like... Oh well, why not. As they sat down at a table Alice spotted friends. 'Look! There's Sébastien and Mirjam. Coo-eee! Over here! Jim was just about to order us all a drink.'

'Thank you, Jim, I'll have a *Perrier tranche*.' Mirjam, being Dutch, pronounced this perfectly – much to Alice's annoyance. Jim looked perplexed. 'Huh?'

'A Perrier with a slice of lemon, Jim. *How* long have you lived here?' She did have a knack of being irritating.

Sébastien tactfully changed the subject. 'Did you hear about the shooting last week?'

Alice looked important. 'Oh yes, we know all about that. Poor Louis. Is he OK?

'Bit shaken up, not surprisingly. But the guy got shot.'

Alice was confused. 'What guy?'

'The guy who held him up,' said Mirjam with exaggerated patience. 'The police set up a roadblock and he tried to get through it. They shot him.'

'Is he OK?'

'No, 'said Mirjam. 'He's dead.'

'Jim and I heard it all, you know,' boasted Alice. Sirens, shots, screams. It was very dramatic. We wanted to go down and see what was happening but Mélodie wouldn't let us.'

Their eyes turned to Jim for confirmation, but he was busy with the paper.

Jean François arrived to take their orders. 'Looks like I'm in the chair,' said Jim, emerging from *Midi Libre*. 'What's everyone having? *Perrier tranche* for Mirjam, coffee for you, Ali? And two *demis* for Sébastien and me. We were just talking about the shooting.'

Jean François knew how to keep his customers happy. 'What shooting?' he asked innocently.

'Didn't you *hear*?' they chorused as one. 'At *La Cloche d'Or* last week...'

'No, it was in the *tabac*, in broad daylight. The robber got away with....'

'No, it was at two in the morning. We saw it all....'

'So what was the *tabac* doing open at that hour?'

Mirjam's clear tones pierced the babble. 'Anyway, the police shot him and he's dead.'

'But we never saw a thing about it in *Midi Libre*,' added Jim, with a hint of regret.

It was too good to resist. Jean François looked at them with a pitying smile. 'Not surprising. It never happened.'

'Oh yes it did, I was there,' Alice was indignant.

'So was I.' replied Jean François. 'It was the day of the St Rémy vs. Montpellier match. St Rémy won by six points. Louis was the hero of the day. We were celebrating all evening, and we ended up at *La Cloche d'Or* in the early hours.

Alice protested. 'But I heard a shot...'

'Oh, that was Lucien. You know, the tall *flic* with the strange moustache? He got a bit carried away and fired his gun in the air. His sergeant has suspended him. I'll get your drinks now.... '

A glum silence descended. Suddenly Alice spied a friendly local: none other than Lucien himself.

'Cooo-eee Lucien, come and have a drink with us!'

Never averse to a free drink, Lucien ambled over to their table. 'Hello everyone. Do you know, I can't believe it. I've just seen Louis.'

'So what?'

'I thought he was dead. Did you hear about the shooting...'

Oops!

La Crémaillère had excelled itself. Karl, Mirjam and Jim sat back from the table with a sigh of contentment. The *daube de biche had* been succulent: tender pieces of venison fragrant with wine and garlic, the *tarte de pommes* glistening gold and just tangy enough, on a layer of crisp, buttery pastry.

'Another glass?' Jim held out the remains of a bottle of *Domaine du Rouge-gorge.'*

'No, I think I'll have a *digestif* answered Karl, summoning Jeanne, who bustled from behind the bar with a bottle of Marc.

'Are you sure you should, Karl?' said Mirjam. 'After all, you have to drive us home.'

'Pooh!' said the big Swede airily. 'The *gendarmes* do not come out till after six, and as for getting home, the old girl knows her way without me steering her.' He glanced affectionately out at the cumbersome Land Rover 110 dwarfing the café's tiny car park.

Mirjam pursed her lips but said no more.

As the trio finally emerged from their lunch in a haze of good cheer, just after four-thirty, the September sun was beginning to make its way down the sky. Mindful that he had taken perhaps a sip or two more than was strictly advisable, Karl Anderssen decided on a circuitous path across the fields to St Rémy. Who knew, a conscientious *flic* might just be on patrol on the main road.

Carefully negotiating the twisting road down from the restaurant, he set off southwest through the vineyards. Progress was slow: the narrow track was rutted and studded with rocks and there was a steep drop on the right. To make matters worse, the late-afternoon sun shone directly through the windscreen.

'I'm blinded: I can't see a thing!' Karl shaded his eyes with his left hand, the right firmly gripping the steering wheel. 'I hope we don't meet anything coming…'

'Look out!' Jim and Miriam shouted simultaneously, as a towering *vendange* machine loomed out of the glare directly in their path.

33

'*Kuk!*' yelled Karl, wildly swinging the steering wheel. The big car served sideways, one front wheel slithered into thin air and they lurched to a stop.

'*Idiots! crétins!*'   Rather than stopping to help, the harvesting machine skirted the stricken Land Rover and went on its way, the driver shaking his fist at them.

'Everyone all right?' said Karl. He shifted into reverse and pressed the accelerator cautiously: the back wheels spun uselessly, and the Land Rover slid an inch further over the abyss.

'Everyone stay where they are,' Karl warned. 'Now, Mirjam, I want you to slide very carefully to your left and get out.'

'If I do that, Jim's weight in the front seat could tip you over the edge.'

Karl sighed – even in a situation like this Mirjam just had to be argumentative.

'Look,' he said carefully, 'Somebody has to go and get help. Jim can't get out because he's on the down side, and if I get out the whole thing could just roll down the hill.'

Strappy sandals aren't made for walking across vineyards, thought Miriam, as she stumbled up the track. In the next field, Louis had halted his tractor to enjoy the fun.

'Louis, don't just sit there like *un con*, Mirjam yelled, 'Come and help us!'

Grinning, the farmer took his time making his way across to the Land Rover.

'There's a tow rope under the back seat, can you reach it?' said Karl, and then, 'Careful!' as Jim squirmed round and hung over the back of his seat.

Surreptitiously, Mirjam reached into her bag, which she had taken care to grab when she left the vehicle. She produced her phone and busily began to take photographs.

Louis attached the tow rope to the Land Rover's bumper and inched his way backwards until all four of its wheels stood on solid ground once more.

'*Un grand merci,*' Karl called as the tractor headed back to the field. 'There's a *pastis* for you in the bar tonight!'

Karl drove the rest of the way to St Rémy tight-lipped with concentration. Something was very wrong. Letting Jim and Mirjam off at the bar, he drove straight to *Garage Dupont*.

'What is it this time?' Gérard, the *garagiste*, was used to Karl arriving on his premises in one dilapidated vehicle after another.

Karl recounted the tale.

'We managed to drive back, but there's something wrong with the steering.'

Gérard tapped the side of his nose. 'Track rods, I'll bet you. Let's take a look.' He disappeared under the bonnet and emerged shaking his head.

'I thought so. I may be able to fix it, but it won't be cheap.'

'It won't be cheap.' How many times, Karl thought, have I heard those words? It must be the first thing they learn in *garagiste* school. He pondered: the 110 really was a bit big for his needs; reluctantly he conceded that he was never going to take off for the wilds of Africa. It was time to sell it and get something more practical.

'How much will you give me for it?' he enquired.

On Karl's birthday, six weeks later, everyone was in on the joke. When the congratulations had been toasted in *Crémant de Limoux*, Mirjam ceremoniously laid a brightly wrapped package in front of Karl.

'Happy birthday,' they all chorused. Inside the package was a picture frame. Inside the frame was a photograph: the Land Rover 110 leaning perilously over the void, one wheel in the air. With uncharacteristic humour, Mirjam had added a caption: 'Oops,' it said.

Karl's new acquisition was an elderly Series 2. Its orange paint had seen far better days, its canvas top was a lacework of holes and one of its deeply recessed headlights lolled like an eyeball half out of its socket. As expected, the Saturday Club were loud in their derision.

'It is a work in progress,' stated Karl, and with great dignity he got up and left the café.

Not much was seen of Karl during the next few weeks, but the dog walkers and the idle curious who happened to pass his garage reported hearing bangs and expletives issuing forth in equal measure from its depths.

At about eight o'clock he would occasionally emerge to join his friends for the after-dinner session at the café, still clad in his ragged and oil-stained jeans. Dominique, the café owner's wife, would tut with affectionate exasperation and rush to place a copy of *Midi Libre* on his chair.

Came the day of the unveiling. It was a Saturday; the market was in full swing and *Le Café de l'Ane* was at its busiest. A diesel roar announced Karl's arrival, followed by the chutter-chutter-chutter of an engine reluctant to switch off. Everyone rushed out to see what was to do.

There stood the Series 2, resplendent in a new coat of orange paint – you could see the brush marks – with a brand-new third-hand canopy sagging over its cracked leather seats, its split windscreen mostly cleaned of flies and other debris. And next to it stood Karl, looking triumphant and a little sheepish in – could it be? – a smart blue suit, dazzling white shirt and a University of Malmö tie.

Accepting a swift *demi* and the congratulations of his friends, Karl dropped his second bombshell. 'Now,' he said, 'who would like to buy it?'

Such was the hubbub of consternation his words provoked that at first no-one noticed the petite, smartly-dressed brunette enter the café. Even in four-inch stilettos she barely reached his shoulder.

As the couple turned to leave, the questions and exclamations followed them.

'Surely you don't want to sell it,' said Mirjam, who always knew best. 'You've spent so much time working on it, and besides you love Land Rovers.'

'That was in the past,' said Karl grandly, 'and as you all know, the past is a different country.'

And, so saying, he lowered himself into the brunette's scarlet Porsche and they drove away.

The News of the Day

At *Le Café de L'Ane*, at the north end of St Rémy's market street, the Saturday Club was in full swing. Today's gathering was larger than usual; the club had spilled out from the cool interior of the café and annexed three of the prime tables under the awning – much to the annoyance of a group of American tourists who had been advancing purposefully on those same tables.

As usual, Jim was holding court. In their little pond he was a big fish indeed: *patron* of the restaurant on the hill above Morbignan, and its resident entertainer to boot. Jim couldn't sing – the verdict on this was unanimous. Jim couldn't play a musical instrument – unless you counted the kazoo.

But Jim was a Performer. Dressed in ragged jeans and a torn Hawaiian shirt, with a glint in his eye and his flyaway moustache a-quiver, he knew better than anyone how to engage an audience. Midnight would come, and one, and two, and still the diners would be roaring out nonsense songs and calling for wine, more wine, while Mélodie, Jim's canny partner and *petite amie*, quietly totted up the bills they never queried.

'So,' Jim raised his nose from his second *demi* and gazed round the table. 'What's the news of the day?'

The news of the day was Horst's dinner party. It was to be a select affair, as they all were. The elegantly tailored German construction engineer had very precise ideas about the ideal number of guests at a gathering. Inez and Gui were among the privileged tonight, but, as usual, sworn to secrecy. On the whole, Horst didn't much care for Inez's Spanish exuberance, but he had a project to discuss with her fussy, wealthy little husband.

'So, who's coming to this bash of yours, then?' said Jim. His sister, Alice, drew in a disapproving breath. Jim winked at her: Horst was notoriously cagey about his guests and Jim delighted in teasing him.

'Those who are invited will know, and those who are not invited will not know.' Horst drew his lips into a thin line, but a slight twinkle in his eyes suggested his enjoyment of the game.

A sudden blaring of car horns had everyone craning to see. *Le Cafe de l'Ane* overlooked the intersection of three roads, at what Jim had dubbed "heart-attack corner". As all the drivers conscientiously applied the French rule of the road – *priorité à moi* (roughly translated as "me first") – this resulted in some exciting near-misses and a lot of voluble Gallic swearing. Today a muddy Citroën 2cv was skewed across the junction and had ended up nose to nose with a Renault van. The drivers were out of their cabs and indulging in synchronised shouting while the backed-up traffic added its horns to the concerto. A red-faced gendarme was trying to sort out the *mêlée*.

Mirjam took advantage of the distraction to leave the table, heading for the *toilettes* at the back of the café. As she expected, Zizi joined her there.

'Do you know who's going tonight?' Zizi wanted to know. It was usually Mirjam who had the low-down on everything.

Regretfully, Mirjam had to deny knowledge. 'But Inez was looking pleased with herself,' she said. 'I'll bet it's them again.'

'Horst's an awful toady,' said Zizi spitefully. 'He always sucks up to Gui because he's got millions.'

'Is he really that rich?' said Mirjam.

'Well how else do you think a fat little toad like Gui got a glamorous Spanish beauty like Inez to marry him? She must be at least thirty years younger than him.'

'*Je m'en fous,*' Mirjam concluded. 'Why do we bother about Horst's silly dinner parties?'

The truth was, everybody bothered. There was a certain *cachet* about being invited, and especially being invited on a regular basis. The elaborate secrecy surrounding the guest list on each occasion was designed to pique the curiosity.

At ten minutes past eleven that night, Horst sat back from the table and beamed at the assembled gathering. This was the best time, he mused, a group of friends well-fed and well-wined, a babble of conversation punctuated with shouts of tipsy laughter. The carefully laid table was now a mess of cheese crumbs and fruit peel, the gold candles had guttered down to stumps, empty or half-empty glasses of *Domaine du Rouge Gorge* were pushed aside as the guests savoured balloons of Horst's excellent *Marc de Banyuls*, the local brandy.

He caught Gui's eye and they exchanged a nod. It had been hard work convincing him, but Horst was persuasive, and in the end money talked: potentially this land deal they had agreed would net them over a million euros.

'Who's for coffee?' Trudi stood up, smoothing the skirt of her Chanel suit.

'How boring was that?' Inez followed her into the kitchen. 'Honestly, all Gui ever thinks about is money. He's already super-rich, but will he spend it on me? I have to beg and plead to buy one little pair of shoes in St Rémy. But he goes on and on about this deal and how much more money he's going to make.'

'Horst is just as bad,' Trudi agreed. 'Oh, he's clever enough, and a brilliant engineer, but with him it's one scheme after another.'

'You know what?' Inez said slowly. 'Someone ought to teach them a lesson. Teach them that they can't always have it their own way.'

'How would we – I mean, someone – do that?'

Inez' eyes were full of mischief. 'This parcel of land they're planning to buy and build on. Suppose someone else got there first?'

'Well, first of all they'd have to know about it. It's not public yet, Horst only knows because he overheard the *notaire* talking to old Madame Martin's nephew. We all thought he was going to take over the vineyard himself, now his aunt's in that care home. She was absolutely determined not to sell, but now it seems she's going gaga and doesn't know her elbow from Tuesday, so Victor thinks he can do what he wants with it.'

'But *we* know, don't we? God knows the two of them have been boring us with it all night. Now say – just say – that someone bought that land out from under their noses?'

'I don't know.' Trudi shook her head. 'Buying the land would be one thing, but it needs massive capital investment.'

'Which we wouldn't have to find!' Inez exclaimed. 'Victor is greedy enough, but I'll bet he doesn't know the true value of that land. Once we have it, we can sell it on to a *suitable* developer for a huge profit.' She winked theatrically and continued, 'Now if one of us were to go and see Victor... I do have a few nice pieces of jewellery that Gui bought me when we were courting...'

'And I still have most of the money from the sale of *mutti's* house,' Trudi broke in excitedly. 'Horst always said I should save it for a rainy day.'

Inez peered out of the window. 'Guess what?' she said. 'It's raining.'

Horst arrived late to the Saturday Club the following weekend. Unusually, Trudi was there before him, giggling with Inez over a *café allongé*. Gui looked on benevolently, stroking his beard like a well-fed cat.

'*Scheisse!*' Horst flung himself into a chair beside Gui. 'We have been betrayed,' he snarled. 'The land has gone.'

'Gone? What do you mean, gone?' said Gui.

'Gone, sold, no longer available. Someone must have got wind of our deal. Who did you tell?'

'Me? I didn't tell anyone,' Gui retorted. 'How about you?'

'I didn't tell a soul. Trudi knew, of course, but she wouldn't... No, it had to be someone at the dinner party last week. Someone I trusted. One of my so-called *friends*.'

'Well I told you we shouldn't discuss business in public'

'You did no such thing. You couldn't wait to boast about how clever we were being and how much money we were going to make.'

The two men glared at each other. Before things could escalate, Jim arrived on the scene.

'*Jour toulmonde,*' he greeted the gathering. 'What's everybody drinking?'

Orders were taken, drinks distributed, the tension dissipated. Jim took a long pull at his *demi*.

'So,' he said, raising his nose from his glass. 'What's the news of the day?'

Inez looked up. 'We do have some news,' she said, exchanging a conspiratorial smile with Trudi, 'but we think Horst and Gui should hear it first.'

Le boute-en-train

Gabrielle sat demurely, plump hands folded in her lap, blushing slightly as the congratulations and compliments exploded round the happy couple. Adam winced as yet another hearty thump landed on his shoulder.

'*Cinquante ans? C'est pas possible!*'

'*Félicitations!*'

'*Quelle bonne nouvelle!*'

The congratulations came thick and fast. Jean-François bustled out to see what was agitating his customers. Mirjam, as usual, had the news.

'Next week is Gabrielle and Adam's 50th wedding anniversary,' she announced. 'Isn't that wonderful?'

The café owner solemnly shook hands with the old *vigneron* and his wife and went off to pour them a celebratory drink on the house.

'So what's the plan?' Jim wanted to know.

All eyes turned to Simon. Jeannette counted quietly to herself: 'One, two, three…'

'Why don't we have a party?' said Simon.

Jeannette turned away to hide a smile. Did Simon ever *not* begin a sentence with 'Why don't we…' she wondered.

Everyone thought of Simon as Mr Fix-it when it came to parties. It was Simon who thought up the idea of a communal Indian supper in the bar, supplied by the local take-away. It was Simon who presided over barbecue feasts in the summer and dress-up-and-bling parties on New Year's Eve. No-one's birthday, new baby or new job went un-celebrated if Simon had anything to do with it.

'*C'est un vrai boute-en-train*, a real live wire.' said the locals, when invited to mingle. He was the life and soul of the party.

Gabrielle looked dubious when Simon approached her with his plan. 'Oh, no thank you, Simon,' she demurred. 'It's very kind of you, but I think we will just have a small lunch for family and close friends at the *mas*.'

(Gabrielle and her husband had retired to a tiny farmhouse in the foothills of the Cévennes, a good 40 minutes' drive from St Rémy, along stony roads twisting up through vines and *garrigue*. If you visit them,

41

you'd be wise to hitch a lift with Karl Anderssen in his 4x4, or with Louis in his time-tested Renault Fourgon.

Arriving at their three and half hectares, be prepared for an exuberant welcome from the three dogs, Roméo, Philandre and Chou, and an eye-watering handshake from Adam. The goose will hiss, but he's a big softie: hiss back at him and he will swiftly retreat. Gabrielle will emerge, smiling and wiping her hands on an apron; delicious smells will follow her out of the kitchen and you know you will be invited to feast.)

'You have your lunch,' Simon agreed, 'and we'll have a party for you in the *Salle des Fêtes* in Morbignan. All your friends want to congratulate you, and you just haven't got room for everyone at your place. We'll have the party on the Saturday after, from lunch time onwards, so everyone can come along.'

Slightly bemused, the old couple found themselves agreeing to the plan. Simon on a roll was unstoppable.

Simon held a council of war in *L'Estaminet*. Marie Claire left Bernard to mind the bar and came to sit at the table. Zizi, Simon's wife, was there, along with Jim, Jeannette, Joséphine and Alice. An hour went by. Empty coffee cups and wine glasses accumulated on the table. Heads nodded wisely, someone produced a notebook, someone else a calculator. At one point Marie Claire disappeared to check her stores.

Jim would run the entertainment, that was a given. No party was complete without Jim, his band and his kazoo.

'Richard will write a song for them,' Simon said. He's good at that sort of thing.'

'And I'll do the music,' said Jim, studiously ignoring the eye-rolls from the assembled gathering.

'You'll do the bar, won't you Marie Claire?' Simon's enthusiasm was at fever pitch. 'And we'll need to organise the food – Joséphine, you know about that sort of thing, don't you?'

By the time the group dispersed the party was planned to the minutest detail. Everyone knew his or her task and set about it with a will: Gabrielle and Adam were well-liked in their community. Not one of the party planners voiced the thought that was uppermost in their thoughts: 'We've all got jobs, but what is Simon going to do?'

What Simon did was to go into a huddle with Joséphine, the mayor's secretary, and book the *Salle des Fêtes*. Then he disappeared.

'Have you seen Simon?' became the regular greeting over the next few days, as the party planners compared notes.

'I need to know how many are coming.' Joséphine complained.

'Have we got mikes and amps organised?' Jim wanted to know.

'Perhaps we will need extra seating? There are only 50 chairs in the *Salle des Fêtes*,' said Jeannette.

Even Zizi was at a loss. 'He doesn't talk to me about it,' she shrugged when they tackled her. 'He just says, "You know what to do, you're brilliant at parties" and then he disappears back into his study. He's working on the computer but he won't let me see what he is doing.'

All became clear three days later, when Simon emerged, triumphant, with a sheaf of posters he had created on his computer. They were a wonder to behold: on a sunshine yellow background he had created a party explosion: balloons, cakes, hearts, wedding rings, fireworks in every hue of the rainbow. In the middle was a large, shimmering gold number 50.

'Come one, come all!' he had written, 'To celebrate the 50th wedding anniversary of our dear friends Gabrielle and Adam!'

The posters went up in the bar, the *épicerie*, the *boulangerie* and on the notice board in front of the *mairie*. Simon had even fly-posted a few crumbling walls in the old town when no-one was looking. The whole village was invited to the party.

There was one tiny problem. It was Zizi who had to break the bad news: '*Chéri*, the date on the posters is wrong,' she said, as gently as she knew how.

Simon was indignant. 'No, it isn't. The 20th is their anniversary. I checked twice with them to make sure I got it right.'

'Yes, *mon chou*, quite right. The anniversary *is* on Tuesday. But the party is on Saturday. The 24th. It was your idea, after all.'

Corrections were hastily made with a magic marker. Although a few bewildered souls did turn up at the *Salle des Fêtes* on the 20th, everybody eventually made it to the party. It was a rip-roaring success.

Almost a hundred guests assembled to wish Gabrielle and Adam well, and the table set aside for presents overflowed with brightly-wrapped parcels.

Marie Claire had overseen the seating: tactfully, she had set two long tables for the French guests, who liked it that way, and a dozen smaller round ones for the English. As the party progressed the lines were blurred: several members of the English community gravitated to the French table to chat to friends, while a few bold French souls were even to be spied sitting at the despised round tables.

Jim and his band belted out all the old favourites and then, on a call of 'Sshhh!' Joséphine, in whose portly frame resided the soul of a true *chanteuse,* stood up and sang the *Chanson pour Gabrielle et Adam* composed by the village's resident poet, Richard Patterson.

At the end of it, the old man was in tears. Despite cries of 'Speech!' and '*Allez, mon gars,*' he shook his head, and instead processed round the room exchanging handshakes and *bisous* with his friends. Gabrielle, made of sterner stuff, managed a '*Merci, mes amis, merci'* before she too was overcome and disappeared behind a large handkerchief.

'That was an excellent party,' said Jeannette, as they settled on their terrace for a last glass of wine before bed. 'It was so good of Richard to write that song. You know, he gets paid thousands for a lyric back in England. He's actually quite famous.'

'But he's a good sport,' said Henry, 'and he likes Adam and Gabrielle.

'I don't seem to remember Simon doing much, though, apart from designing posters and getting them wrong. We were the ones who had to run around the village correcting the date with an indelible marker.

'Gabrielle and Adam brought extra chairs from the *mas.* Joséphine organised a kitty and bought the food, and as I recall Zizi cooked it. Marie-Claire ran the bar and Penny spent hours decorating the *salle des fêtes* with balloons and streamers.'

'Are you surprised?' asked Jeannette. 'We all know Simon. He's great at thinking up ideas, and even greater at getting everyone else to carry them out. When Simon says, "Why don't we?" you know perfectly well he actually means, "Why don't you?"'

'That's all very well, and we all know what he's like,' countered Henry. But what really rankles is that, at the end of it all, everyone told *Simon* what a wonderful party it had been!'

Jeanette shrugged. 'Yes, *chéri* you're quite right. But, after all, he is *le boute-en train*!'

The Rumour Mill Turns Again

Saturday, a hot and dusty market day in late August. In the *Café de l'Ane* the rag-tag band of expats and ne'er-do-wells who comprise the Saturday Club are once again assembling for the weekly gossip-fest.

They bustle into their seats, disposing around and under their chairs their carrier bags of peaches and onions, their baskets laden with *fromage de chèvre* and *saucisson*, their clandestine and rather greasy paper bags concealing the Vietnamese delicacies they are strictly forbidden to consume in the café.

Alice arrives first as usual, rushing to bag the big table by the window. Horst and Trudi enter with Mirjam – they red and flustered after shouldering their way through the tightly-packed tourists, Mirjam cool and elegant and slightly supercilious, as ever. Next comes Alice's brother, Jim, all a-puff from the long slog up the steep market street.

They look round hopefully for Jean-François, but the café owner is busy with a party of camera-festooned Japanese tourists on the other side of the room.

'Good heavens, there's Louis,' Jim remarks suddenly. The Frenchman ambles up, his customary smirk clinging to the grimy stubble of his face.

'*jour toulmonde*,' he greets them. 'Say, did you hear about the shooting?'

They look at him, boot-faced. Trudi turns pink, Mirjam studies her exquisitely manicured nails. Horst rattles his *Midi Libre* in a "don't bother us with your nonsense" kind of a way while Alice plays the "deaf old lady" card and starts a lively conversation with Jeannette at the next table.

There had been a... shall we say a *misunderstanding* the previous year when they all thought someone was dead – Louis, as it happened. It turned out in the end that someone had shot at someone and Louis had seen it. Alice, of course, had claimed eye-witness kudos. It was not, they tacitly agree, their finest hour.

Louis stands enjoying their discomfiture, but just as he is about to launch into the punchline of his little tease, Jean-François comes to take their orders.

'*Salut tout le monde*. Mmmwah! mmmwah!' He greets the ladies with a kiss, the men with a hearty handshake.

'Say,' he continues, 'did you hear about the shooting?'

They can't believe their ears. Is Jean-François, their friend and ally, in on the joke? Is he in cahoots with Louis after all? Just as Jim is beginning to splutter, Jean François goes on:

'Yes, it's true, there's going to be a shooting, in this very café, next Thursday! They say George Clooney himself is coming, but I doubt it. It will probably be a stand-in.'

Realisation dawns. A shooting? A *film* shooting? Exciting news indeed, or rather it would be, were they not such world-weary sophisticates.

But there's more.

'You could all be in it if you want,' the café owner assures them. 'I spoke to the location manager, he wants extras to be sitting in the café while the scene is being filmed.'

They look at one another and solemnly shake their heads. No, they rarely if ever meet in St Rémy on a Thursday: Saturday is their day. Alice has promised to cook her famous poached salmon for Elise and Danny's 25th anniversary party. Horst and Trudi are on standby to help Antoine with the *vendange* – his famous Merlot grapes are always picked early.

So, of course, on Thursday morning the little café is largely empty. Only Jim can be seen, tucked into a corner table at the back of the room, engrossed in his day-old *Guardian*. Alice arrives by chance: she has had to come into St Rémy to book a chiropodist appointment. She greets her brother with surprise and agrees to stay for a quick coffee. She is wearing a smart jacket – after all, one can't go into the *cabinet* of a medical professional looking like a bag lady.

Karl Anderssen, self-styled retired linguistics professor from Malmö, lives in St Rémy, so everyone is used to his dropping in to the café after a morning spent at the library. Seeing Jim and Alice already there, Dr. Anderssen decides it would be churlish not to join them. As he sits down, Mirjam emerges from the *toilettes* at the back of the café. Being Mirjam, she does not condescend to explain her presence in St Rémy on a Thursday. She is wearing a new shade of nail polish.

One by one they all troop in, each looking slightly sheepish, each with a plausible excuse. It's been raining, say Horst and Trudi, so Antoine won't pick the grapes until the weekend. Marie Claire's son has come home unexpectedly and she needs to buy *saucisse de Toulouse* for the cassoulet she is making him – apparently her village butcher doesn't stock it. All of them are looking remarkably spruce and well-kempt.

They decorously order coffee and Perrier – it wouldn't do to be seen imbibing alcohol at this early hour.

The only person missing is Louis. Is he embarrassed at having teased them so cruelly? Does he feel he doesn't deserve to be in their number? No, wait: there in the distance they see him coming, unshaven, his blue dungarees stained with some nameless filth: clearly, he hasn't made the effort. And he isn't alone. Lurching along in his wake are 'Jules et Jim', octogenarian goat farmers from *Le Mas Germain*. Their grimy berets squat toad-like on their greasy brows, redolent as usual, no doubt, of goat and manure.

And – wonder of wonders – here comes the camera, dollying backwards as the grunge brigade advances. They are coming to film! In the café! Spines and jackets are straightened, hair discreetly patted.

Then Jean François comes over to the group with a studiously downcast face.

'I'm sorry,' he says, 'but you have to leave now. The producers need the café for their filming.'

This is indeed a bombshell.

'But…' Horst splutters. 'You told us…'

Mirjam cuts in: 'You said we would be needed as extras for the scene.' Jean François's apologetic *moue* is convincing – almost.

'They want real "characters", peasants, men of the soil,' he explains.

'So why did you get us all in here when we have better things to do?' This from Jim, who is beginning to go purple.

Jean François shrugs. It is a Gallic shrug. An elaborate shrug. A caricature of shrugs. 'Well, you know,' he says, 'business is always slow on a Thursday…'

PART TWO

MORBIGNAN TALES

Of Vines and Wines and the Prospect of Babies

Morbignan la Crèbe, a small village in the Languedoc.

Population, winter: 673¾. Marie-Helène is expecting her third in a few weeks' time.

Population, summer: 1,200-plus, when the owners of the *maisons secondaires* descend from England and Germany and Switzerland, and the families visiting rural parents arrive in time for the July 14 festivities.

Principal industry, winter and summer: gossip.

Secondary industry: wine.

The old town is a jumble of ancient stone-built houses nestling within a crumbling Roman wall, for Morbignan can claim a long and venerable history. Walk up through the narrow cobbled streets, where scarlet geraniums spill from half-barrels at every doorstep; here the old ladies sit on hard kitchen chairs to observe the world as it passes by. Pause by the ramparts to gaze out over the river, La Crèbe, torrential in winter, where the coypus play in the water and assemble with the ducks under the stone bridge for tourist titbits.

Gaze up at the heights of *Le Mas Germain*: if your eyes are good you may glimpse 'Jules' or 'Jim', octogenarian goat farmer, herding his flock towards a ramshackle milking parlour. Look down and you will see the patchwork of vines at your feet. It is September, and the grapes hang plump and ready for the *vendange*.

In years gone by Languedoc was not famous for its wines. For years, the hundreds of tonnes of grapes that yielded by its grudging soil were shipped off in industrial containers to bulk up the cheap wines that France, with typical Gallic cynicism, sold to her overseas neighbours.

'*Les Français adorent le Piat d'Or*' cajoled the British television commercials of the eighties. And only in the privacy of their richly-furnished offices did the advertising executives allow themselves to snigger:

'*Les Français ignorent le Piat d'Or.*' The French know nothing of Le Piat d'Or.

Morbignan's own *Domaine du Rouge-gorge* was the jewel in the crown of the *cave coopérative*. Of smoothness, bouquet and mellow flavour *Rouge-gorge* was entirely innocent. It was cheap, you could say

51

that, and it had a satisfying hangover-inducing kick that the hardiest among the villagers found appealing and the rest of the population treated with wariness.

Indeed, Lola de la Lune, the *ancienne belle* who lived with her cats in a tiny, crooked house in the *rue des merles*, would often remark; 'The good thing about *Rouge-gorge* is that if you drink it at a fête you can use the leftovers to take your nail varnish off.'

Then came Jose Hernandez, Spanish refugee from the turbulence of the 1930s. He bought the *domaine* from old René Marceau and set about revitalising the crop. His son, Manuel, picked up the baton in the late 1970s, and with his inspired blend of Syrah and Merlot grapes produced a prizewinning wine. The words *Médaille d'Or* were proudly affixed to the label and Morbignan was, viticulturally speaking, on the map.

Now, on this bright September morning, retired *vigneron* Gaston Bergerac sighs with contentment as he reflects on the season to come. The best time of the year, he thinks: the season of wine. The *rentrée* is over – that mad scramble to get the kids back to school and the populace back to work - and all the incomers have gone. The blasting heat of July and August has mellowed to a golden autumn warmth. The grape harvest, the *vendange,* is under way.

The roads around Morbignan are perilous with towering *vendange* machines – tall, thin crane-like things that look as if they might topple at the slightest puff of wind. They are specially designed to fit between the tightly packed rows of vines, harvesting the grapes for Morbignan's famous vintage. The velvety dark-red wine has just won coveted AOC status and the village holds its collective head just that little bit higher.

Just like every morning, at seven sharp - no need for an alarm clock - Gaston is up, washed, dressed, shaved and ready for the day.

Gaston is a man who loves his routine. A widower, with his four children scattered across Europe, Gaston lives a contented and resolutely independent life in the ugly, inconvenient three-storey village farmhouse he moved into as a young married man.

Each morning he walks the few steps to the *boulangerie* for his *baguette*, returning home to breakfast on his tiny front terrace overlooking the street. From here he looks down benignly as his neighbours pass on their various errands. Everyone has a kind word or a friendly greeting for the upright little man, with his faithful hound Maître at his feet.

'*Bonjour* Monsieur Bergerac.'
'*Bonjour* Madame Duval.'
'*Salut* Gaston!'
'*Salut* Jean-Pierre.'
'*Quelle belle journée!*'

Breakfasted, with the crumbs scrupulously brushed from waistcoat and moustache, the coffee cup washed up, Gaston installs himself in the village square. There an immense plane tree stands, circled by a wooden bench, its green paint cracked and peeling. Every one of the *copins* (cronies) has his allotted place.

Davide, the former *maire* of the village, is the first to arrive, with Jolie skipping beside him. By Gaston's reckoning this is the fourth in the line of Jolies, stretching back to the days when he and Davide would spend their mornings chasing rabbits in the woods and their evenings chatting up the girls in the café.

Jolie (pretty one) is a Brittany, a typically French hunting dog, tan and white with silky ears and a stubby tail which she wags constantly. Every twelve years or so there are tears, and Davide is missing from the bench for a few days. After a suitable period of mourning, another Jolie will be introduced to the group under the plane tree and receive her quota of cuddles and coos.

As Davide begins the ritual of lighting his pipe, Kiki swaggers up. Kiki is the teenager of the group – he can't be more than 60 – and his *enfant terrible* reputation glows about him like an aura. Kiki went dancing last night. They are agog: who did he escort home? Who prepared his morning *café*? Kiki smiles and winks mysteriously: he's not telling.

One by one the rest of the gang assembles: P'tit Gui the builder, glancing round to make sure no customers are pursuing him; Matthieu the plumber and Jim, honorary Frenchman, who runs the restaurant up on the hill. Surrounded by his cronies, Gaston whiles away a tranquil morning with pipes and gossip, until it is time to go home for lunch: usually bread, an odorous hunk of *saucisson* or a yellow wedge of cheese, perhaps a modest glass of wine.

Today, as on every Friday, he treats himself to lunch at the café. Marie Claire greets him with affection: they have been carrying on a stately flirtation for the past five years. She sets before him *Salade de chèvre chaud*, glistening with olive oil and aromatic with fresh herbs, followed by *filet de perche* with ratatouille. He disdains dessert, settling for a small, strong black *café*.

'It's tomorrow, isn't it, *mon chou*?' says Marie Claire, as she pauses by his table. 'Jeannette and Henri are here for the holidays?'

Gaston's beam lights up the room. 'Yes, tomorrow. And they're bringing the baby!'

Marie Claire's expression struggles between delight and fury. 'Jeannette had a baby? And you didn't tell me?'

'*Non, ma belle, pas un bébé-bébé*,' Gaston placates her. 'They have a new dog, a sheepdog puppy. I am so looking forward to meeting her.'

'And to seeing your daughter,' Marie Claire reminds him.

'Oh, yes, of course I am looking forward to seeing Jeannette and Henry,' says Gaston, and can't resist adding:

'And the baby.'

A Dog Called Useless

At home in south-west London, Henry Prendergast opened one eye and wondered why he felt so elated. It wasn't that he usually woke up depressed: no, working for Glenwood Publishing was still a buzz after almost 18 months - but this was an unusual level of cheerfulness even for a Saturday.

Beside him, Jeannette stirred, then turned and grinned. 'It's today, *chéri*,' she mumbled through a cloud of dark hair.

Today! Of course! Henry tumbled out of bed and raced to get to the shower first.

'*Auprès de ma blonde...*' he bellowed tunelessly as he splashed, so that Useless, who had come up for her morning cuddle, whimpered and put her paws over her ears.

'It's off on your hols you are, my gorgeous one,' he told her. Useless wagged happily. You'd think she knew she was going to France today, to meet *papa* for the first time. Of course, Henry told himself solemnly: in her case it would be *grandpère*.

The Old English Sheepdog puppy had come into their lives rather unexpectedly six months ago, in March, and immediately turned everything upside down. Owning – or, as Henry sometimes thought to

54

himself, being owned by – a large, happy, lolloping, grinning bundle of grey and white fur certainly made life... interesting.

One of the problems with the pup was that she just loved everyone. Show her a burglar and she'd lick him to death. Show her a sheep and she'd want to play with it. She was, as Henry was wont to point out, useless. Useless as a watch dog and useless as a sheepdog. Despite Jeannette's protests: 'She's got a perfectly good name of her own,' the nickname stuck.

Now, after a flurry of vaccinations, a microchip and a lot of paperwork, she was the proud possessor of a Pet Passport, complete with cute photo. And today she was about to put her paw on French soil for the first time.

The trip to Morbignan la Crèbe was something they looked forward to all year. Jeannette's father, Gaston, still lived in the little village in the Languedoc where Jeannette had grown up. Every September, like homing pigeons, they returned there.

Seven hundred miles away, in Morbignan, Gaston Bergerac woke with the same sense of happy expectation as his son-in- law. Today Jeannette and her husband were coming to stay, and bringing the new baby. On the whole, Gaston approved of the fact that the baby was grey and white and fluffy rather than pink and squalling. As a grandfather of seven he was blasé about small humans, but dogs he loved.

He wondered, though, how Maître would respond to an interloper. The old hound had served him faithfully in the days when they used to go hunting. Now they were both older, man and dog preferred a stroll in the woods. There was always the hope of finding a small truffle to take home. Maître, like Gaston, was partial to a truffle omelette, and he was becoming quite useful at nosing out these delicacies.

As evening fell, the Prendergasts' car drew up, almost filling the tiny street. Gaston needn't have worried about Maître's reaction. No sooner had Useless exploded from the car, all tossing hair and flirty bum, than Maître capitulated. It was love at first sight.

Jeannette and Henry spent the next day settling happily into familiar routines. They took Useless on their favourite walk: down the steps behind the church and along the riverbank. The little path across the river, studded with uneven stepping stones, was dry. To the left, the remains of the river lapped gently in a swathe of grasses, while to the right it lay still in tepid pools. Later in the week, as tradition demanded, they would bring their picnic down here, enjoying their cheese and *saucisson* mid-stream.

'I can't believe that in a month or so the water will be roaring over these stones,' Jeannette mused. 'I must take a photo of our picnic, and then get Papa to take another one at the same spot in January, for comparison.'

Henry laughed. 'Are you aware that you say that every time we come here in the summer?'

Turning for home, they panted up the slope through the vineyard, laughing as the village dogs rushed to pay homage to the pretty newcomer. Useless preened and pouted and flirted.

'Takes after her *maman*,' Henry remarked. 'A real French tart.'

They stopped at the café for a pre-lunch drink. Marie Claire, the owner, greeted them delightedly. 'How well you look, how you've...' she stopped just short of the comment. Jeannette was no longer a child, to be complimented on how big she had grown.

'How you've been missed,' she amended, rallying. Jeannette giggled – plenty of the good ol' boys in the square hadn't been so tactful.

Gaston had prepared a *cassoulet* in their honour and opened a bottle of *Domaine du Rouge-Gorge*. After such a feast, a siesta was the only possible option, and the afternoon passed in a pleasant, drowsy haze.

The following morning Gaston proposed a treat: a truffle-hunting expedition.

'It's a little early in the year,' he told them, 'but I have been lucky in September before.'

Jeannette and Henry exchanged a dubious glance. The same thought was in both their minds: Useless, rampaging through the woods, scaring the wildlife and distracting Maître from his serious duties?

'Well,' said Jeannette, 'if you're sure.'

'Quite sure,' said Gaston firmly, and Maître gave one sharp bark of assent.

Henry Prendergast was bewildered. 'Truffles? I thought they only grew in the Périgord.'

Gaston regarded him indignantly. 'Not at all, you English philistine. Some of the finest truffles come from the Languedoc.'

Somehow they all crammed into the old man's battered Peugeot pick-up with the dogs in the back, and set off for the woods.

'Maître has become an excellent truffle hound, you'll see,' said Gaston proudly. 'I think I can promise you a wonderful omelette for your supper.'

Maître had other ideas. All he wanted to do was show off to his new girlfriend. He darted here and there like a puppy, seeking out the most delectable smells for her enjoyment, flushing an unwary rabbit, leading her to a stream for a little refreshment.

Suddenly, Useless stiffened. Her nose came up. Her tail came up - and she ran. Within seconds she was out of sight, lost among the tall trees. Jeannette panicked.

'She doesn't know these woods. She'll get lost and we'll never find her.' She was almost in tears.

Gaston, who had been sulking somewhat at his hound's lack of prowess, suddenly saw a way to redeem the family honour.

'Find her, Maître, good boy, find her,' he commanded.

The old dog bounded into the woods. Five tense minutes passed, then came an explosion of excited barks and yelps. Following the sound, they came to a small clearing with a tall oak tree in the middle. Maître stood there, wagging and barking frantically. There seemed to be no sign of Useless, until they spotted a plumy tail waving from the bottom of an immense hole at the foot of the tree.

'Useless,' Henry commanded. No response. 'USELESS!' He used his 'I really mean it' tone of voice. Slowly the tail dipped. Slowly, reluctantly the puppy backed out of the exciting hole.

'She has something in her mouth,' said Gaston. And then, with a gasp, '*Mon dieu!*'

Proudly the pup laid her trophy at her master's feet. It was black. It was the size of a small orange. Even from a distance it gave out a pungent, earthy smell. Gaston bent and picked it up.

'It must weigh almost 100 grams,' he said with awe in his voice. 'Do you realise, this truffle could fetch anything up to 50€ on the open market?'

There was a gleam of triumph in Jeannette's eye as she turned to her husband.

'So? Do you still think she's useless?'

'Not at all,' said Henry. He bent to stroke the dog's silky ears. 'What a clever girl you are,' he said.

Later that evening, the family relaxed on the terrace. With a fragrant *omelette aux truffes* and a bottle of the excellent local white wine inside them, they were in mellow mood. It was what the French called *l'heure bleue*, that languorous half-hour after the setting of the sun. The swifts, which had been shrieking their heads off, dive-bombing round the church tower like demented stukas, were at last settling to roost. The first bats fluttered out into the blue dusk.

Smiling lazily over at Useless, who lay entwined with Maître in a fluffy heap, Henry remarked:

'You know, it's time we found a proper name for her. We can't go on calling her Useless for the rest of her life.'

'I know,' replied Jeannette, 'but her kennel name, "Silverleaf Daddy's Delight", is just too awful.'

'Why not call her after a famous huntress, like Diana,' Gaston chipped in. 'After her prowess in the truffle woods she deserves such a name.'

Jeannette pulled a face. 'Oh, Papa, you know I hate human names for animals.' She paused, then inspiration struck: 'Of course, we could call her Artemis, it's the same thing, only in Greek.'

'Yes,' added her husband enthusiastically, 'and then we can call her Missy for short.' Jeannette shot him a look, and he subsided.

And to this very day, whenever an unsuspecting friend asks why their pretty dog has such an unusual name, Henry and Jeannette exchange a glance. 'Well,' one of them will begin, 'it's like this…'

Cheeky

The little village of Morbignan la Crèbe was on tenterhooks.

In the café, several of the regulars huddled at a corner table, talking in whispers, their *Midi Libres* pushed carelessly aside, their *cafés* cooling at their elbows. Bernard, the barman, was keeping a wary eye on the door. Occasionally he glanced at the baseball bat tucked under the counter, each time giving himself a little reassuring nod. If trouble was coming, he was ready.

Everybody jumped as the swing doors were flung open, and on a roar of '*Ou est-il donc?*' Sylvestre shouldered his way into the room. Drifts of sawdust clung to his tattered dungarees and there were twigs in his dishevelled hair. Lightly, almost disregarded, at his side swung the axe of his trade.

'*Ou est-il donc?*' (Where is he, then?) he repeated, glaring suspiciously round the small café. Bottoms shuffled on hard chairs, eyes were cast downwards: no-one would meet his bloodshot stare. No-one was in any doubt whom the irate woodsman was looking for: it had been the talk of the village for weeks. Kiki had been up to his old tricks.

By rights Kiki should have been among them: normally you could set your watch by him. Every day at 11 am *pile* he made his entrance, dusty from his labours in the vines, ready for his *café allongé* with just a teeny-tiny *Marc* on the side. With a familiar cry of '*Jour toulmonde!*' he'd stand in the doorway of the café, his thumbs hooked in the pockets of his skin-tight jeans, windblown hair raked back with casual fingers. With a wink for the ladies and a nod for the men, Kiki had arrived.

Kiki was the village's oldest teenager. Never mind that he had seen more summers than the most venerable wines in the *cave coopérative*. Never mind that no small amount of grey now threaded the once-lustrous black locks. Never mind that he was soon to be a grandfather for the third time: in Kiki the glory years lived on.

The English members of the community, not surprisingly, called him Cheeky. The ladies of the village adored him. The single, the celibate and the widowed among the male population enjoyed his stories and his escapades. Husbands and boyfriends viewed him with a certain distrust.

Today was different. Today there was no Kiki at his usual table, no shouts of laughter dominating the conversation, no tall tales to hold everyone spellbound with delight or disbelief.

And, even more telling, the *tabac* was closed. This was unprecedented: every day from 11:15 to 4:30 (apart from Sundays and *jours fériés* of course) Kiki was to be found at his post behind the counter, dispensing *Midi Libres* and Marlboroughs and cheap novelties for the tourists with a friendly word and a saucy grin.

'*Ou est-il donc?*' Where was he, indeed? And – the unspoken question hung in the air – where was Paulette? Sylvestre's mousy little wife hadn't been seen in the village for a couple of days. She had, it's true, recently been spending more time in the *tabac* than the occasional purchase of a newspaper warranted. She had, it is also true, been taking an early morning stroll in the vines of late, once her husband had breakfasted on *café au lait* and a hunk of fresh *baguette* and gone about his daily rounds. Had something been Going On? With nods and winks and wise taps to the nose, Morbignan concluded that something had.

A week went by, and two, and nothing was heard of Kiki or Paulette. The villagers travelled to St Rémy or the nearby village of Les Herbes for their tobacco fix. It was after one such quest that Jim returned with a tale to tell.

'While I was out, I thought I'd swing by Cap d'Agde and check out the new bistro. Thought I might get myself a gig.'

Matthieu and P'tit Gui exchanged a glance. Typical Jim, they thought, but did not say.

Jim was the village's *Monsieur Showbiz*. He and his girl frind Mélodie ran the restaurant on the hill above Morbignan, *La Truite Dorée*. And Jim was the resident entertainer. No, he couldn't sing. No, he couldn't play any musical instrument save the kazoo – and that he played badly. No matter: Jim was a performer: he knew how to get an audience on its feet and stamping wildly with approval. Sometimes, with Guitou on the harmonica and Jeannine on the double bass, he would persuade an unwary café owner to give his "band" a late-night spot.

'I dropped into the *Café du Port* while I was there, and who do you think I saw? Kiki!'

'Kiki? What was he doing?'

'How did he look?'

'Did he recognise you?'

'Did he say anything?'

'Was Paulette there?'

'How did she look?'

'Did she say anything?'

Jim raised his arms protestingly under the hailstorm of questions.

'Yes he recognised me, yes he looked fine, yes Paulette was there, yes she looked fine, yes he said something. He said "*Bonjour*". Paulette looked more than fine, actually, I hardly recognised her. She's had her hair done and she was wearing make-up.'

"Shhh!' Matthieu raised a cautionary finger. It was too late. Sylvestre had come in, unnoticed, and was listening quietly to the conversation. Without a word he turned and strode out of the café.

'Oops,' said Jim.

If the habitués of *L'Estaminet* expected the woodsman to return dragging his prodigal wife by the hair, they were in for a surprise. Sylvestre was missing for a day or two. When next he walked into the café he did, indeed, have a woman on his arm. It was not Paulette.

As usual, Jim had the lowdown.

'I was just finishing a set at *Le Chat Noir*, that's that new bistro I told you about, and blow me down if Sylvestre didn't walk in with this bit of stuff. She can't have been more than eighteen, but she had so much make-up on it was hard to tell. Very cosy they were, too.'

'*Ce qui va pour l'un,*' remarked Davide from the next table. The former mayor had a tendency to be pompous.

'Yes, sauce for the goose! Good on him,' Jim agreed, and winced as Mélodie kicked him sharply under the table.

'Well?' he countered. 'She went off with Kiki, didn't she? Sylvestre's got a right to have some fun.'

'*Ou est-il donc?*'

The summer evening was soft and they were gathered on the terrace of *L'Estaminet* for a pre-dinner aperitif: P'tit Gui, Jim, Mélodie, Alice, Matthieu, Richard (also known as P'tit Mat) and Gaston Bergerac.

The woman erupted through the café doorway on six-inch stilettos and stood, arms akimbo, glaring at the assembled drinkers. Her sun-streaked blonde hair was swept back in an elegant *chignon*, discreet make-up enhanced her deep brown eyes and her designer suit perfectly outlined a figure that set Jim's eyes gleaming.

'*Mon dieu!*' gasped Alice. 'It's Paulette.'

'Yess, eet's Paulette,' she mocked, 'And where ees my 'usband?'

'At home, I imagine,' ventured Jim, 'But, Paulette…'

Turning on her heel, she was gone.

The group looked at each other. Very casually, Alice rose. 'Well, must see about getting dinner,' she muttered as she set off in Paulette's wake.

'Wait up, Alice, I wanted to ask you…' Jim was right on Alice's heels.

One by one the drinkers rose from the table and drifted, as if absent-mindedly, in the direction Jim and Alice had taken: the direction of Sylvestre's house. Paulette had disappeared inside.

For a long time, all was silent, then, on a crescendo of shrieks, the door was flung open. There stood Sylvestre, looking sheepish. And there stood Paulette. In her hand she had a fistful of bottle-blonde hair with a struggling, protesting 18-year-old attached.

'And don't come back!' With a flick of her elegantly-shod foot Paulette sent the interloper sprawling into the road. Noticing her audience, she raised her chin with a challenging stare.

'*Eh bien, quoi*?' she said, and slammed the door in their faces.

Sylvestre was a man transformed. He stood straighter, walked with a jaunty step, greeted even the most casual acquaintance with a vigorous handshake and a bellowed '*Bonjour, chef*!' Every evening would see him stride into the café with Paulette by his side, settling her into her chair with the proud solicitousness of a new lover.

Paulette wore her crown lightly, but never once did she relinquish the upper hand.

Kiki was rarely seen in the village after that.

An Honorary Good Ol' Boy

Henry Prendergast was an Englishman; there was no getting away from it.

No matter how hard he tried to blend in, how conscientiously he learned his French idioms, how much he cooed over babies in the square, to the villagers of Morbignan he was always '*l'anglais.*'

He wore jeans and a T-shirt, they saw a pin-striped suit and a bowler hat. He said: '*Bonjour Madame,*' politely when he encountered a neighbour in the *épicerie*. Madame said 'Good morrrneeng' with kind condescension and tutted to herself about his atrocious accent.

True, he had a French wife, and that was a point in his favour. True, he was not slow in standing his round in the café – and that, if truth be told, was even more greatly in his favour. But *l'anglais* he was and would remain, it seemed, forever.

And of course, it was the Good Ol' Boys who decreed his status.

Every small French village has them: the good ol' boys who congregate in the village square or in the bar, gossiping and swapping tall tales and passing comment on the world as it goes by.

Morbignan is particularly blessed in good ol' boys, Gaston Bergerac among them. A dozen or more can be seen of a morning, whiling away the time till midday when Madame calls them in for lunch. It's always *midi* on the dot, of course – an hour which Henry, in honour of the local accent, calls '*l'heure du paing et du ving*' (the hour of bread and wine).

They have their favourite spots, the good ol' boys, and woe betide anyone who trespasses without invitation. The main gathering place is on the circular bench under the big plane tree in the *place de la mairie*. Others prefer the benches that line the road, or the shady square by the post office with its war memorial and fishpond.

Three in particular liked to park themselves, on drowsy afternoons, on the bench next to the old-fashioned metal bottle bank. Henry had his own theory about why they favoured this noisy spot.

'They do like to trot out their jokes,' he would report back to Jeannette after a trip to dump the latest consignment of empties.

'They have two. One is: "Hey! Don't wake us up!" and the other is "You can leave any full ones with us." '

Henry, who knew his place, would laugh dutifully and shake the proffered calloused hands with enthusiasm. His standing with the Good Ol' Boys rose a little higher each time, but still he was *l'anglais*.

And then one day it all changed.

Jeannette had had to fly back to England on some errand or other, leaving Henry and Gaston, her father, to a peaceful masculine camaraderie. The village was celebrating one of its many traditional *foires* and Henry strolled out to see what was going on, taking the video camera with him.

He was doing his best to be inconspicuous, but the good ol' boys have antennae for that kind of thing. Soon they were playing to the camera for all they were worth.

That evening Jeannette got an excited phone call. Henry's French, it seemed, which was still pretty basic when she was there to translate, amazingly blossomed into fluency when she was not. 'And we had a really good chat,' he burbled, 'and guess what: they invited me to sit on the bench with them!'

Jeannette knew her wifely obligations. Here was clearly a case for unbridled enthusiasm. 'Well done you!' she congratulated him. 'You've cracked it: you're an honorary Good Ol' Boy!'

Visitor

PFFFFFT!

A streak of black-and-white shot across the kitchen as Banjax hurled himself underneath the dresser, where he crouched, glaring defiance. His brother, Bandicoot, uncurled himself from the hearth, languidly stretched one back leg, then the other, and strolled out to see what was to do. He touched noses politely with the small brown and white mongrel wagging hopefully on the doorstep, then turned and miaowed imperiously at Richard.

'Hmm?' Richard Patterson was immersed in *Midi Libre.* 'Well, if that's Visitor you had better invite her in.'

'Did I hear Visitor's name?' said Martha, coming into the kitchen. Wisps of damp silver-threaded auburn hair escaped from her towel turban and snagged in the three silver rings she wore in her right earlobe.

Richard put down the paper.

'I think she likes it here. She gets a lot more cuddles than she does at home, I imagine. Not to mention the treats,' he added severely, as Martha reached for the bag of dog biscuits she kept in the kitchen drawer.

'If she *has* a home,' Martha said. 'I keep asking around the village, but nobody seems to know who her owner is. I asked Kiki the other day and the cheeky so-and-so said, "Isn't she yours, *Madame?*" If we go on like this, we'll end up keeping her, you know.'

Richard sighed. The little dog was now sitting at his feet, one paw on his knee, gazing up at him with mahogany brown eyes.

'Help, Martha, she's "doing cute" again!' he protested, ruffling the dog's ears.

'But we've been over this a million times. In the first place, she probably does have a perfectly good home of her own. You can see she's well looked after, and she isn't exactly thin – that can't all be down to the treats you slip her when you think I'm not looking. Secondly, what about the cats? Banjax would probably leave home, and then there'd be another stray animal wandering around Morbignan.'

'Bandicoot likes her,' Martha objected. 'And you know what a wuss Banjax is. He'd soon get used to a dog around the place, especially if he thinks his big brother is in favour. Besides, I've never known a cat who didn't rule the roost. Remember Nero?'

Her husband grinned. Their friends Annie and Marcel had an enormous dog: Martha swore he was half carthorse.

'Lucky for me he's a big softie,' Richard would say, as once again Nero stood on his hind legs and enthusiastically licked his face. Nero's favourite place was the Papasan chair which stood in a corner of Annie and Marcel's conservatory; he would curl up in it, head lolling and paws spilling out in all directions. It looked excruciatingly uncomfortable, but woe betide anyone who dared to claim the chair when Nero wanted it.

Then Annie acquired a kitten. Even by kitten standards she was small, a scrap of tabby fur. Annie excitedly described the new member of the family to her friend over coffee and croissants, but Martha was dubious.

'How on earth are you going to keep Nero away from her? He could swallow her in one mouthful,' she said.

Annie winked. 'Come over tonight for *apéros* and you'll see.'

That evening, as they walked into their friends' apartment, Martha and Richard could see Nero curled up in his favourite chair in the conservatory. Normally he would bound over to welcome them with big wet kisses, but that evening he seemed strangely reluctant to leave his spot.

'Where's the kitten?' said Martha.

'You'll see,' Annie said. She opened the kitchen door and the little cat strolled out. Ignoring their coos and coaxing fingers it trotted straight through to the conservatory and stood looking up at Nero. It mewed: one short, peremptory mew. Nero whimpered, looking imploringly at Annie. No help was forthcoming. The kitten mewed again, and with a mournful sigh the big dog heaved himself off the Papasan chair and slunk away into a corner. The kitten leapt, catching the edge of the cushion with its claws and scrabbling to haul itself up, then curled itself into a ball and went to sleep.

Richard laughed, remembering. 'You see?' said Martha triumphantly. 'You can't tell me that two big strapping cats can't get the better of one little dog?

The summer wore on. Every two or three days the dog would arrive on the Pattersons' doorstep, a happy grin on her face, one paw raised in mock entreaty. Richard would pretend to be stern, shooing her away with unconvinced hands. Visitor know how to deal with that one: she simply rolled on her back, paws waving wildly, and dared Richard to resist scratching her belly. Martha was a much softer touch: the moment the little brown and white face peered round the kitchen door, Martha was reaching for the treats.

And still the debate continued: shall we keep her? There was no doubt in Martha's mind. Richard played the stern pragmatist as hard as he could, but his wife noticed his objections were increasingly feeble. Even Banjax stopped running for cover whenever Visitor appeared; if he thought no-one was looking he would come over cautiously to touch noses.

'Allo! 'Allo! The loudspeaker at the top of the church bust into a rapid gabble.

'What was all that about?' Richard's French was sketchy at the best of times, and the trumpeted announcements that came from the church tower always defeated him.

'I'm not sure, I wasn't listening,' said Martha. 'Just wait a minute.'

Sure enough: *'Je répète,'* said *Allo! Allo!* and the whole announcement was duly repeated.

'Oh, of course, it's the Fourteenth,' said Martha. 'It's on Saturday night: we'll have to go and get our tickets at the *Mairie.*'

'Or what?' said her husband. They looked at each other and laughed. Every year it was the same: *Allo! Allo!* would be heard at increasingly frequent intervals with ever more frantic demands that the villagers go and collect their *billets* for the grand feast of July Fourteenth. There would be a barbecue, it announced, and *moules marinières*, and more wine than you could shake a hangover at, but only, *only* if the tickets were collected by close of play on the Thursday before the *fête*.

Of course, the good people of Morbignan took not a blind bit of notice until the very last minute. Just before six p.m. on the Thursday, a long queue would snake out of the *Mairie* and around the corner, past the *tabac* and the *épicerie*, past the *boulangerie* where Gaston Leblanc jeered from behind the evening *baguettes*. Somehow everyone got their tickets, or else they were let through on the nod, because not a soul was missing on the night of the *fête*.

The culmination of the evening, after the feast and the dancing, was always a grand firework display. Usually these were let off in a nearby field, which meant a perilous trek down a stony path, the ladies in their party-best high heels slipping and slithering and clinging to their escorts.

This year was different. As the assembled revellers were preparing to move, standing up, shaking out their skirts, gathering up the plates and glasses, there was a sudden 'Whoosh!' followed by a loud bang. Right in their midst, half a dozen rockets flared up into the night and sparkled down in cascades of silver and blue and green.

'Aaaah,' went the crowd, in time-honoured fashion, but Martha was distracted. She had seen what others had not: a brown and white streak as Visitor shot across the square, ears flattened, tail tucked between her back legs.

'Look!' Martha clutched Richard's arm in dismay. 'It's Visitor. She's terrified. We have to go look for her.'

Richard was disinclined to move.

'She'll be fine: this happens every year, she must be used to it. Watch the fireworks.'

Martha was quiet, uncharacteristically so. As Richard turned to her, sparkles from another cascading firework glinted in the moisture on her cheek.

They searched for an hour, but they could find no trace of the little dog. At last, reluctantly, they returned to the square for a final drink before turning homewards. The lantern was lit in their porch; in its light they saw a small, shivering shape pressed hard against the front door.

'That confirms it,' Martha said later, as Visitor settled herself more comfortably in her lap and put out a sleepy pink tongue to lick her hand. 'She is ours now.'

Visitor made herself at home with lightning speed. Within days, it was as if she had never lived anywhere else. Richard and Martha she ruled, as Martha put it, with a paw of iron. Her ears were her best feature, and she used them shamelessly. If Richard tried to tell her off, if Martha said 'no' in her best 'I really mean it' voice, Visitor would simply look at them, brown eyes limpid, head cocked to one side and her wide, fringed ears standing out in a glamorous bouffant that Richard called her Tina Turner look.

With the cats, Visitor came to a cautious accommodation: Banjax continued to regard her with some suspicion, but Bandicoot was more than happy to curl up and cuddle together on the hearth. She was happy, confident, affectionate, irresistibly pretty – and a confirmed thief.

It wasn't long before the Pattersons realised that the new member of their family had a pathological obsession with food. Anything she was offered, she ate. Anything she wasn't offered, she stole. And, for a small dog, she had an amazing reach: more than once Martha had found her parading the kitchen on her hind legs like a meerkat, scoping the worktops for anything inadvertently left vulnerable. Soon a new expression entered Richard and Martha's conversation: as they tidied away a meal one of them would remark,

'Make sure you put it out of small-furry-nose range.'

But however hard they tried to thwart her, Visitor was determined. The kitchen waste bin was her favourite target: all sorts of good things lurked in there. The bin was behind doors in a cupboard under the sink, but that was no problem. Cupboards were made to be opened, and it wasn't long before Visitor learned how.

Richard tied the cupboard handles together with an elastic cord. 'That'll stop her,' he thought, and soon he was bragging about his cleverness to friends whose dogs had similar bin-raiding tendencies. This lasted until the day Martha went back to England on a short visit. Richard took her to the airport, leaving Visitor at home, with all surfaces bare of food and the waste bin secure behind tightly bungee'd doors.

'You will not believe this,' Richard told Martha later on the telephone. 'When I got home, she had only managed to get the cupboard door off its hinges.'

'Oh, dear,' said Martha, striving to sound appalled, 'did she get into the bin?'

'What do you think? I found her sitting in the middle of the kitchen floor with rubbish strewn all around her. She looked exceedingly pleased with herself.'

'Did you tell her off?' Martha wanted to know.

'Of course I did, severely,' said Richard, grateful that, on the other end of the telephone, his wife couldn't see his fingers crossed behind his back.

Not everything required theft or cunning, though. With her film star looks and cajoling ways, Visitor was past mistress at softening the hardest hearts. Old village ladies who, up till then, had sternly ignored the English incomers, now stopped to coo at the dog and chat about the weather. The mayor slipped her sugar cubes under the table in the café, despite Martha's protests.

The *boulangerie* was Visitor's favourite spot. They would pass it every morning as they came back from a walk by the river, and every morning Visitor would pause as the rich scent of buttery baking warmed the street. Invariably the baker would trot out with a morsel of croissant or some other delicacy and pay his tribute to the pretty dog.

One morning she went walkabout. They had returned from the early walk and Martha was busy in the kitchen, with the front door open to the warm summer air. Visitor settled down to snooze on the tiny front terrace, but when Martha glanced up she had disappeared.

Martha wasn't too worried. After all, Visitor had been a street dog for at least some of her life. Every now and then the old ways would surface, and she would wander off; she knew every inch of the village, everyone knew her and would keep an eye out for her.

Ten minutes later she was back. Martha looked at her in horror: in her mouth was a large freshly baked croissant. Grabbing her purse, Martha rushed down the road, Visitor skipping at her heels.

'*Pardon, Monsieur, pardon!*' Martha gasped as she entered the *boulangerie*, and indicated the dog, grinning happily around the croissant still clamped in her jaws. '*Je paie.*'

'*Non, non, Madame, c'est un cadeau.* A geeft. I give 'im to 'er because she is so *jolie.*'

Martha looked at Visitor. The dog looked back at her.

'What?' said the cocked head, the ears akimbo. 'What?'

Chickengate

Oh, dear, he's grinning again,' Heloïse Dubosc said to her husband. The latter, Maurice, was sprawled at ease on a sun lounger at the far end of the terrace.

'So? You know the drill: grin back at him.'

Heloïse laughed. The trouble with these old houses, she reflected, charming though they were, was that their layout led to some confusion, to put it mildly. Under Napoleonic law, inheritances were stringently divided, and this led to some quirky real estate solutions. To the left, the Duboscs shared a party wall with their next-door neighbour but one.

To the right was the home of Gaspard Petit and his long-suffering wife Mireille. They had moved in when the original incumbent, François Peitavy, retired. Peitavy was for many years the village *notaire*, and the house next to the Duboscs was his *cabinet*, or office, not his residence. The first-floor kitchen, which overlooked Heloïse and Maurice's terrace, was dark and unused. The fact that they and the *notaire* were co-proprietors of another house, which stood directly opposite the Duboscs' and opened onto their terrace, was therefore of no consequence. Peitavy owned the *cave*, which by rural tradition was the ground floor, while Heloïse and her husband had the two top floors, which they had turned into a self-contained *gite*.

If Petit had rejoiced in the laid-back, *laissez-faire* attitude of most of the villagers, harmony would have continued to reign in the little street. Alas, he did not. Neighbours to him were anathema, and *foreign* neighbours unspeakable.

For, sad to say, this is what the Duboscs were: foreigners. Heloïse hailed from Clermont l'Hérault, which was bad enough, but Maurice was originally from Lyon. How dared such interlopers presume to settle in Morbignan, where only the children and grandchildren and great-grandchildren of inhabitants could truly justify calling themselves *Morbignanais*?

Oddly enough, none of the other villagers seemed bothered by this heresy. Their attitude to incomers of any variety was simply this: were they *des gens correctes*? Did they sweep their front steps, shop in the *épicerie*, say *bonjour* politely when they encountered neighbours in the street? Once this was established, the village was ready to welcome any new arrival. Even the English were tolerated: Richard Patterson, who was rumoured to be a Poet, and his convivial wife Martha were frequently welcomed into the evening *apéro* circle at *L'Estaminet*.

Gaspard Petit was having none of that. His war against the Duboscs was silent, for the most part and, truth to tell, not very deadly. He had taken to grinning at them from his kitchen window, a bottle of *rosé* grasped firmly in his fist, and seemed rather put out that they were not more frightened by this tactic. More troublesome was the fact that the grimy, cobweb-infested hole – one could hardly call it a window - in the wall of Petit's *cave* looked out onto the Dubosc's terrace stairs.

Looking at him now, as he stood swaying belligerently above her, Heloïse felt a twinge of guilt.

'Do you think we should have warned them?' she asked her husband anxiously.

'Warned who about what?' Maurice was half asleep beneath his *Midi Libre*.

'That nice English family. They love the house, but they have no idea what kind of neighbour they are inheriting. When he finds out they're English, not to mention the other differences, he's bound to kick off.'

'Oh, they'll make short work of him, I'm sure. Have you *seen* the mother-in-law? Hard as nails, that one, if I'm not mistaken. I'm sure she'll know how to deal with *Monsieur Dingue* (Mr. Crazy).

For the Duboscs would soon be leaving the village and the troublesome neighbour behind: they had concluded a satisfactory sale of their house with James Carcenet, an English antiquarian bookseller, and they were moving to the pretty town of Agde to be nearer their daughter and her young family. In ten days' time they would be hosting one final farewell gathering, to which friends and neighbours were all invited.

The day of the barbecue it rained. Of course it did.

'It never fails,' thought Heloise, setting out knives and forks and counting wine glasses. 'It can be the longest, hottest summer on record, but the moment you plan a barbecue and invite a dozen of your friends... it rains!'

It was a typical Midi thunderstorm. The sky at noon turned black, the rain hurtled down, lightning and thunder rolled around the sky as if it would never cease. Heloïse wasn't too worried: these weather tantrums soon blew themselves out, And, sure enough, by six o'clock the terrace was dry and Maurice was lighting the barbecue; at seven o'clock the guests started to turn up.

First on the doorstep were Maître Peitavy, accompanied by his wife and his luxuriant moustache, and his special crony Thierry the *vigneron* with his tribe: wife Céleste, daughters Dominique and Zara and assorted husbands, boyfriends and small people. The terrace was already beginning to look quite full.

Next to arrive were Richard and Martha Patterson and Bernard and Lili Durand.

'I see Monsieur 'I-have-farted' is here. First as usual,' Patterson said to his friend. Durand looked nonplussed.

'What is this?' he enquired.

Patterson laughed.

'It's a Latin joke, though probably not a very accurate one. '*Péter* in French means to fart, yes? *J'ai pété* would mean "I have farted". I simply took the Latin construction – "avi" -- to put it into the past tense: pét-avi"

Durand, whose school Latin had scarcely gone beyond "Amo, amas, amat," laughed politely.

'Really, these English are *very* strange,' he thought to himself.

The meat was beginning to sizzle on the grill, sending up enticing aromas of wood smoke, garlic and herbs; the guests gathered hopefully round the barbecue, clutching plates already laden with fragrant salads.

'Ware Chickengate!' Heloïse said to her husband.

Patterson, the inveterate wordsmith, was intrigued.

'What on earth is Chickengate?' he wanted to know.

Heloise and her husband looked at each other and burst out laughing.

'The dreadful tale begins on an evening much like this one,' Maurice began. The guests edged closer: Maurice was famed for his storytelling.

'It was a family barbecue; Lisette, our daughter, had come to stay for a few days, with her husband Paul, their three-year old and the new baby. Our son Gérard had brought his girlfriend along for the first time. Lisette is particularly fond of grilled chicken, so that is what we were having.

'Perhaps unwisely, I had set up the barbecue in the shade, which at this time of the evening is at the far end of the terrace, just by the steps down to the wood cellar. The chicken was nicely done, and I was just lifting the first portion with my tongs when calamity struck. Daniel, the toddler, was running about as toddlers will, and he cannoned into my legs. I was caught off balance, I staggered, the chicken flew from my grasp and...' He paused dramatically.

'It fell. It rolled. It bounced off the first step. It bounced off the second step. And then it flew... right in through the window that you see there. The window of Gaspard Petit's *cave*.'

73

The guests were reaching for tissues and paper napkins as the tears of joy rolled down their cheeks.

'We didn't know what to do,' Maurice continued. 'Petit doesn't go into his *cave* very often. Should we say nothing? Should we just leave the chicken there to fester? We couldn't do that, not even to our obnoxious neighbour. So...'

'We wrote him a note!' Heloïse burst in. 'We said we were very sorry, that it was an accident, but perhaps he should know...'

'He never responded,' Maurice took up the tale again. 'We don't even know if he got the note or read it if he did. Perhaps that chicken leg is lying there still.'

Howls of laughter greeted this. Several people clutched their stomachs, doubled over with glee. Suddenly Heloïse sobered.

'Watch out!' she hissed, looking up.

Silent above them stood Gaspard Petit at his kitchen window. Silent, brooding, glowering down at the assembled guests. As they followed Heloïse's gaze, Petit spat an obscenity and shook his fist at them. Then he slammed the kitchen window shut.

'Oh, dear,' said Heloïse. 'That does not bode well.'

As events transpired, she was to be proved right.

The boy in the water

She was just another summer visitor, that's all the villagers knew. She had rented Germaine's house from the old lady's son-in-law, after Germaine had decamped to Montpellier to be near her sister.

Morbignan accepted her – she smiled at her neighbours in the street, sometimes sipped a *pastis* in the bar on the square – but no, no-one could say they really knew her.

It was three weeks into her stay at the little house in the vines when something woke her one night. The gecko on the wall blinked and scuttled away as she switched on the bedside lamp and padded barefoot to the window. The night was rich with cricket song and the far-off, monotonous *bip* of the scops owl. The pool was a bright splash: she must have forgotten to turn off the lighting. Minute insects danced above its surface and there was a rustle in the bougainvillea as some night creature slipped away, disturbed by her presence.

A movement caught her eye. The boy was playing in the pool, swimming like a dolphin, his movements graceful and silent. One of the village children, she supposed. She watched him for a long time as he swam and luxuriated in the silky water. Then she went back to bed.

The next night she sat out late, as the hammering sun finally dropped into the blue dusk, as one by one the screaming birds ceased their circling of the rooftops and settled to roost, as the first bats fluttered out into the thyme-scented night. And still she sat on; locking up around midnight she was careful to turn off the pool lights, standing for a moment as her eyes adjusted to the summer night. Above her the stars swept across a clear sky, the moon a silver fingernail-paring low on the horizon.

The illuminated face of the clock said two when she woke. She listened, straining her ears, but there was nothing. The window, which should have been black in this deepest hour of the night, was washed by a ghost of grey. She knew before she looked out what she would see. The boy's lithe form was silhouetted by the soft blue lighting of the pool as he swam and turned and dived, frolicking and joyful.

75

In the morning she quizzed Josiane, when the pretty teenager from the village brought her croissants and a local paper.

'Who is the boy who comes to play in my swimming pool at night?' Then, as the girl's smile vanished, she added, 'No, don't worry, I'm not angry. He looks so happy, playing in the water. I'm just puzzled. Who is he, and how does he turn on the lights when I am careful to turn them off before bed?'

The girl put the croissants on the table, took her few coins, bobbed a 'Merci Madame', and fled.

'Merci Madame.' The old man stood on the terrace in the blasting noonday sun. In his hands were an earthenware crock of olives, a small jug of wine, a few wildflowers.

'I don't understand,' she said. She stepped back, inviting him into the cool of the shuttered salon. 'I don't understand,' she said again, pouring a glass of fresh lemonade for each of them.

The man shrugged.

'We don't understand, either. Why should it be you he visits? But we accept, for you too are part of the village. It is water he loves, a well, a stream; but your pool would have tempted him beyond resistance. Don't be angry, don't be afraid, those who see him are blessed.'

'But who is he?' she wanted to know. 'Where does he come from? He must have a home, a mother?'

The old man shrugged again.

'I don't know Madame. None of us knows. He is simply the boy who plays in the water.'

Boar wars

'Allo! Allo! Le traiteur de St Laurent, Maison Dupuy, est installé sur la Place avec tomates farcies, saucisses aux lentilles, gardiane de taureau...'

The residents of Morbignan la Crèbe collectively reached for their purses. Here was an eagerly-awaited treat: the mobile deli from St Laurent had arrived in the market square with, among other delicacies, the first *gardiane* of the season. This rich, wine-infused stew of beef, chestnuts, mushrooms and herbs was a speciality of Maison Dupuy. It followed hard on the opening of the *Feria* season: the region was close enough to the Spanish border to allow an overspill of the barbaric custom of bull fighting.

The English in the community, at least, preferred not to know whence came the meat for their *gardiane*: it was a guilty pleasure but an irresistible one, and soon a queue would form in the village square as Monsieur Dupuy, red-faced in the confines of his mobile catering van, doled out the delicacy in half-litre tubs.

Matthieu, though, had other things on his mind. Partial as he was to a *gardiane*, its appearance also marked the opening of the hunting season. This year, he told himself, this year...

The tubby little plumber had one burning ambition: to bag himself a *sanglier,* a wild boar. Season after season Matthieu, along with P'ti Gui, Gaston Bergerac and Jean-Marc from the *cave cooperative* would don their camouflage gear, dust off their shotguns, whistle up their dogs and set off on the quest. First, though, there would be the ritual *paing et ving* as the hunters fortified themselves with lunch and a glass or two before setting forth. It was not so surprising, therefore, that despite the impressive armoury piling up on the pool table in *l'Estaminet,* despite the boasting and the backslapping, nothing ever came of it.

Wild boar there were a-plenty in the *garrigue*, the scrubby hillside surrounding the village, but never a one did they manage to shoot. Other things did end up in the swag bag: birds, rabbits, even the odd unwary goat. Dogs regularly came in for a sprinkling of shot, which was why those that survived were reluctant to accompany their masters and had to be bribed with morsels of chicken liver filched from the midday salad.

Even the hunters themselves were not immune, and many a one staggered home in the evening with a wound or two.

'Well, what do you expect?' Marie Claire would say, pouring another round of consolatory *demis* as they trooped back to the bar in the evening. 'You tog yourselves up in camouflage jackets but those boars are so short-sighted they couldn't see you even if you were wearing bright red. All it does is make you invisible to humans.

'Then you let fly at anything you see moving in the bushes and you're surprised when you shoot each other? It's a good job that shot you load your guns with is so feeble.'

An English tourist sparked a frenzy of excitement one evening. She was overheard confiding to her husband that she'd seen a small boar in the garden of a house near the *cave co-op*. Alas, it was only a large dog: the tourist, it turned out, was exceedingly short-sighted.

Two days later, when Matthieu came home for his midday meal, his wife reported: 'You've had a call-out from Jim at *Le Mas Germain*.' Matthieu groaned. The ramshackle goat farm was run by two elderly brothers. Lost in the mists of time were their real names: everyone, including the brothers themselves, referred to them as Jules et Jim. Every now and again, when a drain overflowed, a thrice-patched pipe burst or a dripping tap became a torrent, the brothers would grudgingly call on the services of a plumber.

Le Mas Germain sprawled in the hills above Morbignan, a good three quarters of an hour's drive up a steep and rutted track. Matthieu knew he was in for a long and tiresome afternoon struggling with Jules et Jim's parsimonious attempts at plumbing, followed by weeks of threatening and cajoling until the bill was finally settled.

It was nearly six o'clock when Matthieu bade farewell to Jules et Jim, after thanking them effusively for the glass of water they had granted him after his labours. Sarcasm was lost on the brothers, who stood smiling benignly as the plumber climbed wearily into his Peugeot van and set off down the road.

Milou had been asleep on the back seat. The orange and white spaniel raised his head, whining for a caress. Matthieu reached back and scratched him behind the ear and the old dog subsided happily, his head on his master's shoulder, wuffling moist contentment into Matthieu's ear.

The track rounded a clump of olive trees and dived into a steep turn. Mathieu sighed with pleasure: this view was one of the few rewards of the unrewarding visits to Le Mas Germain. A patchwork of small vineyards spread out at the bottom of the valley; he could almost see the neat rows of vines, with their clumps of scarlet geraniums at each end, the grapes beginning to plump up ready for the *vendange*.

Only Louis' field spoiled the happy symmetry of the vineyards. As usual, it was a shambles: weeds rioted between the rows of vines, which still sported the long *sarments*, or suckers, which should have been trimmed back weeks ago. A pair of gnarled olive trees marked the boundary. Unusually, Louis himself was in the field, an awkward shape crouching between the rows.

Or was it Louis? Matthieu caught his breath. Could it be? He cut the Peugeot's engine, letting gravity take him freewheeling down the stony path. At the bottom he braked and stepped out of the van, Milou at his heels. Louis' patch was near enough for Matthieu to get a good look.

It was! A large, black boar was snuffling through the vines, trampling the laden plants underfoot.

Shaking with excitement, Matthieu reached into the van for the shotgun which always travelled with him. Gesturing to the dog to be silent, he crept forward. When he judged the distance right, he took careful aim...

The moment he fired he realised his mistake. In his rush to bag the *sanglier* he had neglected to check the cartridge: the gun was loaded with 2.2 shot, which was quite sufficient to wreak havoc among the local rabbits. It was no match for a boar.

Hearing the shot, the animal raised its head. Something had scratched its left shoulder and it was not best pleased. Its piggy eyes peered myopically in the direction of Mathieu, who by now was backing away, raising his hands as if to propitiate the beast. An unfortunate gust of wind chose that moment to blow across his shoulder and right into the enraged face of the boar. Scenting the enemy, the boar lowered its head. It pawed the ground once, snorted and charged.

A peeved boar can easily overturn a small van; the only safety lay aloft. As Matthieu sprinted for the nearest olive tree, an orange and white streak told him that the dog had chosen to save his own skin, never mind fronting up to half a ton of angry pork.

As Matthieu would later relate to an enthralled audience, the beast's hot breath was at his heels as he leapt for the lowest branch of the olive tree. Perhaps this was a teeny exaggeration, but Matthieu was never one to let a few facts spoil a good story. Be that as it may, the plumber managed to haul his not inconsiderable weight to safety. He looked at the boar.

'*Vas t'en!* Shoo!' He flapped an encouraging hand.

The boar looked back at him. It huffed. It pawed the ground again and then, to Matthieu's horror, it lay down at the base of the trunk.

Night settled round the adversaries. The boar stretched with a sigh, then rolled on its back, scratching luxuriously in the stony soil. It flumped down on its side and began to snore.

Mathieu crept cautiously down the trunk. Something loomed in the darkness: two little red eyes glinted malevolently an inch from his nose. Time froze, then Mattheiu shot back up the tree faster than he would ever have thought possible.

It was a long night.

Josette wasn't too worried when Matthieu didn't come home that evening. He had probably got involved in one of Jules et Jim's interminable poker games. She hoped he hadn't lost too much this time. At ten o'clock the next day she strolled over to the café. Her husband was sure to be there, looking bleary-eyed and sheepish, fortifying himself with a strong *café noir* before going home to face the music.

No, said Marie Claire, setting out a basket of croissants on the bar; no, she hadn't seen Matthieu that morning. Josette began to worry. Had he had an accident? Was he lying on the road with a broken leg or, god forbid, a broken neck? Milou, she knew, would have stayed with his master: the dog hadn't the wit to go and fetch help.

Richard wandered into the café.

'*Hola, 'ti Mat, bonjour!*' Josette greeted him with relief. Her son scowled at her.

'*Maman*, I've told you, my name is Richard. Don't call me Petit Mat!'

'Never mind about that. It's *Papa*. He didn't come home from *Mas Germain* last night and there's no sign of Milou.'

'So what?' said Richard. 'You know *Papa*. He'll have been playing poker with the old boys and Milou will have spent the night snoring by the fire.'

Josette wasn't convinced. 'They'd have been back by now in any case. You'll have to go and look for them.'

'Well let me have my coffee first,' grumbled her son. 'And then I'll go.'

Ten minutes later Richard climbed into his rusty Citroën pickup and set off in the direction of *Mas Germain*. It wasn't long before he spotted his father's van, the door swinging open and Milou curled asleep on the back seat. He stopped. There was no sign of Matthieu

'Pssst! Richard!' Richard looked around: his father's voice seemed to be coming from an olive tree.

'*Papa!* What on earth…'

Olive branches agitated wildly.

'Stop! Look, can't you see?'

There was a large black shape at the foot of the tree. As Richard peered at it, it raised its head and stared a challenge at him.

'Ah. *Un moment, Papa.* Don't move.' Richard extricated a box of heavy-duty cartridges from his glove compartment and loaded his shotgun. One clean shot and the boar rolled over, dead.

Relief and fury struggled to gain possession as Matthieu scrambled down. Saved by his son, what a hero! Thwarted of the first boar of the season by his son, what a traitor! In the end, good sense and good manners prevailed.

'*Merci*, Richard, that was an excellent shot,' he said through gritted teeth.

Between them the two men manhandled the carcase into the back of Richard's pickup.

'Let's take it to Marie Claire,' Richard suggested. 'She can get it butchered and then make us one of her wonderful *daubes de sanglier*.'

Mattheu pulled a face. 'You know, son, I've rather gone off *sanglier*,' he said.

The Poet, the Thief and the Indian Prawn

Martha Patterson opened the door and stepped into the kitchen bursting with excitement and news.

'Rick?' she called. There was no response from her husband, and no sign of him. He wasn't, as she had expected, sitting in the *salon* by an early log fire, a glass of wine in his hand and Visitor entwined with Bandicoot on the hearth. He wasn't upstairs on what they rather grandly called the Minstrel's Gallery - the first-floor landing - catching up on the latest instalment of *Breaking Bad* on their old and capricious DVD player.

She shook the rain drops from her cloak and hung it on the hook, pausing to run her hand over its fleecy softness. Summer was glorious, she thought, but there was a special savour to autumn, when the tourists had gone home, the nights were drawing in and a wood smoke scent drifted through the streets of Morbignan as the residents lit their first fires.

She finally ran her husband to earth in his little cubbyhole off the terrace. Formerly an outside toilet, they had converted it a year or so back into an office for Richard. The broadband was patchy but sufficient for emails and the odd bit of Googling his research required.

'Working, love?' She poked her head round the door. Richard sat back from the computer and pushed his glasses up his nose for the hundredth time that evening.

'Hm?'

Oh, dear: she knew the signs. Still, against all experience, she persevered.

'Guess what, we're getting a takeaway.'

'Hm?' Richard looked confused. 'I thought you left a *daube* in the slow cooker.'

Martha gave up, temporarily. The news would wait until supper, when she could claim at least a quarter of his attention.

'Yes, I did,' she soothed. 'Supper in ten minutes.'

'Er...' His eyes had strayed back to the screen; his fingers did little ghost-taps, straining to be back on the keys.

'Ten minutes, remember,' Martha sighed and went to lay the table.

Martha was a foodie. She loved food: talking about it, reading about it, experimenting, devising recipes. And she was a superb cook. As she switched off the slow cooker and took off the lid, rich, fragrant steam caressed her. This one would be a triumph, but Richard would never know.

Oh, he'd make the right noises.

'This looks good,' he'd say when she served his plateful. And, 'That was delicious,' he would pronounce, trying to disguise the fact that he was itching to leave the table.

But she had to face it. Rick was seriously not interested. Just her luck, she thought, to be married to a non-foodie. But then, that was par for the course. She and Richard were diagonal opposites: if he liked something she was sure to hate it, and vice versa. He often jokingly referred to them as Jack Sprat and his Wife. Perhaps it was their differences that had kept them together for nearly thirty years.

'How was your evening?' Richard asked as they sat down.

'Great' Martha had recently joined *Le Club du Troisième Age*, a French version of the U3A, and she was a leading light of the amateur dramatic group.

'We're going to do Agatha Christie this Christmas.

Richard had his confused face on again. 'In English?'

'No, silly, in French. She's been translated into just about every language on the planet, you know. We're doing The Mousetrap – *La Souricière* – and I'm going to direct.'

Richard smiled at her fondly. Just like Martha, he thought: she's been here ten minutes and already she's into everything. It freed him up for his work: he hated spending time apart in the evenings, but when she was out at one of her groups he could shut himself in his study and wrestle with rhymes to his heart's content.

Everyone in their community knew that Richard Patterson was a poet. When he and Martha joined the crowded table at the Saturday club in St Rémy, Horst would be sure to sing out, with heavy humour and muddled linguistics, '*Achtung, tout le monde, hier kommt der Poet'*. When Richard walked down to the *boulangerie* for their morning baguette, Gaston Leblanc would greet him with a wink and a '*Bonjour, monsieur le poète'*.

The only person who did not subscribe to this notion was Richard himself. 'I'm not a Poet,' he would demur, his voice implying the air quotes. 'I'm a humourist, a versifier, if you will.'

This modest claim belied the fact that Richard Patterson was an in-demand comic writer; he had published five successful books of verse that still sold well on Amazon, and was working on a sixth. He was regularly called on to provide verses for newspapers and television, and he contributed a weekly limerick to a satirical magazine. The commissions paid well and contributed to the comfortable lifestyle they now enjoyed in France.

'Now, what's all this about a takeaway?' he said, remembering his manners. All too often his eagerness to share his own news overrode anything she wanted to tell him.

'Remember when *Chez Isolde* closed?' said Martha. The rival café had never taken off: the villagers much preferred *L'Estaminet* – after all, most of them had gone to school with Marie Claire, its owner, while Isolde was an incomer.

'Yes, that place has been empty for more than a year,' said Richard.

'Well, it won't be empty much longer. We're getting an Indian restaurant! And I was talking to P'tit Gui this evening – he's playing the policeman, he's going to be brilliant – and he swears that it'll do take-away. Apparently Gui's cousin is going to manage it.'

'Splendid,' Richard said. 'It's such a bore having to go into St Rémy every time we fancy an Indian and, let's face it, the *Tandoori Mahal* there isn't very good. Let's hope they get a good chef. Now…'

Martha bowed to the inevitable: his attention was slipping again. With a smile, she asked the question he had clearly been longing to hear.

'Are you working on something new?'

'Yes, it's a parody. I think it's going to be rather fun. I was over in the bar earlier this evening and I bumped into Jack.'

'Jack Fletcher, that tall streak of nothing who looks as if he lives half his life on a sunbed?'

'That's the one. And I've told you before, his grandmother was Greek, that's why he looks so tanned.' Martha rolled her eyes but said nothing.

'Anyway, he had a book with him, a copy of *Alice in Wonderland*. I was leafing through it and I found this wonderful poem, something about a white knight sitting on a gate…'

'Yes, I know it,' Martha interrupted. 'It's actually in *Through the Looking Glass*. You know it's a parody too, don't you?'

Richard looked nonplussed. '*Through the Looking Glass* is a parody?'

'No, *it* isn't, but the poem is. It's a take on a poem by Wordsworth. Lewis Carroll said so himself.'

'Oh. Anyway, I was crossing the square on my way back and I saw all the Good Ol' Boys sitting under the big tree, and the Worm bit.'

The Worm was what Richard called his sudden flashes of inspiration, and when it bit him, as it frequently did, all he could think about was getting to a piece of paper or a computer screen and writing.

'I could just see it,' he continued, eyes shining. 'It's about the Good Ol' boys and I'm going to call it *A-sitting on a Bench*. Though it's going to be hard to find a rhyme for bench, I think.'

'Seriously?' Sometimes, Martha knew, her husband got so wrapped up in his creations that he overlooked the obvious. 'You live in France and you can't think of a rhyme for bench?'

'Oh.' Richard blinked. 'Yes, well…'

'Off you go,' Martha said, and she started to clear away the dinner plates.

'Shall we spoil ourselves and get an Indian?' said Richard Patterson one Friday evening. It was becoming a regular weekend treat, now that *Monsoon* had opened its doors in the *Rue de l'Eglise*. 'I'll give them a call. What do you fancy?'

'I'll have a Lamb Passanda for a change,' said Martha, 'and get plenty of poppadums.'

There was no need to ask what Richard would have: it was always the Tandoori Mixed Grill. P'tit Gui's cousin Arlette often slipped him an extra tandoori prawn when no-one was looking.

'Look at Visitor!' Martha laughed.

The little dog, who had been spark-out in front of the fire with her best friend, the black and white cat Bandicoot, suddenly sat up and looked alert.

'I swear she knows the word Indian.'

'Why wouldn't she? It's to do with food, isn't it? Well, you're not getting any, Madam: it's bad for dogs,' Richard continued with mock severity.

Visitor settled back down on the hearth, but Martha noticed her ears were at half-mast.

'Oh dear,' she thought. 'Mischief on the horizon.'

The smells were almost unbearably enticing when the take-away was delivered. As Patterson dished up the food, Visitor and Bandicoot were in close attendance and even Banjax, Bandicoot's brother, suddenly appeared to keep an eye on the proceedings.

'Watch out for marauding cats'n dogs,' warned Martha, as they sat down to their supper.

'No chance,' said her husband, tempting Fate. Fate was listening.

They were finishing their meal. As usual, Richard had left his tandoori prawn for last. Suddenly Visitor looked up, growling, the hair on her neck standing up. She rushed to the back door, barking frantically and pawing at the wooden panel.

Richard was on his feet. Someone had been getting into the back garden of late, digging up bulbs and overturning the table and chairs.

'I'll have you this time,' he yelled, and flung the door open. Visitor dashed out between his legs and ran around the garden, still barking.

'I can't see anything out here... hey!' Richard was almost knocked off his feet as the dog sprinted back into the house. He turned in time to see her bound up on to a chair, snatch the prawn from his plate almost in mid-air and hit the ground running. By the time he had gathered his wits, Visitor had disappeared into the cubbyhole under the stairs and was munching, with ferocious delight, on her ill-gotten gains.

'Hey!' he said again, 'I was looking forward to that.'

Martha was shaking, tears running down her face.

'Your little dog is obviously a master of diversionary tactics,' she gasped. 'You should have known better than to trust her.'

'*My* little dog? She's no dog of mine!' Richard was biting back his own laughter as he sat down again. A solitary poppadum remained on his plate; he munched it thoughtfully.

'Still,' he mused, 'What a story it will make. Or, better still...'

Martha grinned. Soon, she knew, Richard would disappear into his study again.

Fire! Fire!

Joséphine was in her element. She cleared her throat daintily and with a plump forefinger pulled the switch towards her. The faint hum of an expectant microphone caused her to nod with satisfaction. With another slight 'Ahem!' she began:

'Allo! Allo! La poissonnière de Thaillac est installée sur la place...'

From the comfort of her cluttered desk on the ground floor of Morbignan's *Mairie,* Joséphine was the voice of the town crier. Whatever went on in the village, it was up to her to document it: lost dogs, found keys, a new menu at *l'Estaminet,* Joséphine had the news and *Allo! Allo!* announced it, from a pair of loudspeakers set at the top of the church tower.

Wednesdays were best. This was the day of the tiny Morbignan market, when five or even six *marchands* gathered in the village square. The butcher, the fishmonger, the *charcutier*, the greengrocer, the stall selling ladies' knickers – all required their wares to be listed in exhaustive detail. Joséphine was up to the task.

It was all thanks to "Papa" Pardieu. The new *maire* had taken office three years earlier. M. Pardieu was an innovator, determined to bring Morbignan into the 20th century, at least – the 21st was perhaps a step too far. He had the derelict buildings of the old winery pulled down (M. Lemaitre having taken his celebrated Rouge-gorge to shiny new purpose-built premises in the hills) and laid a much-needed car park. In earnest pursuit of the title of *village fleuri* he had baskets of flowers hung from every lamp post and set up tubs of marigolds, geraniums and lantanas along the main street.

When Marie Claire petitioned him for permission to build a terrace at the side of *l'Estaminet*, M Pardieu graciously consented. No more would her customers have to sip their coffee at little tables on the narrow pavement in front of the café, risking death from diesel fumes and erratic drivers.

The village was on the map, and it was all thanks to Papa Pardieu. The new mayor had gained his nickname in honour of his six children. How this polyprogeniture had come about was a source of delighted speculation among the regulars at the café: visions of the round, pompous, balding little *maire* engaged in energetic rumpy-pumpy with the cool and elegant Madame Pardieu were almost too delicious to contemplate.

And there was more. Not only did "Papa" have a fragrant, fruitful wife: he also had a *petite amie!* Incredible though it might seem, everybody – apart, presumably, from Madame Pardieu – knew that the mayor was carrying on an enthusiastic liaison with Agnes, Gaston Leblanc's niece, who worked in the *boulangerie* on Thursdays and Saturdays.

'I wonder how he has the time,' remarked Alice on more than one occasion, to which her brother invariably riposted:

'I wonder how he has the stamina.'

To tell the truth, Agnes was a little jealous of Joséphine, who had daily contact with the *maire*, but she needn't have worried. Joséphine had her own *petite amie*: they lived as sisters in her snug little cottage just outside Les Herbes. Suffice it to say they were not related.

Papa Pardieu's latest project was the renovation of the old loudspeakers on the church and *cave cooperative*, and the re-institution of a vocal commentary on village life. In years gone by it had been the *tambour* who roamed the streets of Morbignan with his drum, calling out the news of the day. An enlightened and forward-thinking mayor had replaced him with the broadcast commentary, immediately dubbed *Allo! Allo!* because of its way of announcing itself, but the system had lately fallen into disuse.

Naturally, as secretary to the *maire*, it fell to Joséphine to be the new voice of *Allo! Allo!* She took to the job like a duck to the proverbial; indeed, she looked a little like a duck, waddling round the village with her chin held high. Joséphine was, in her own mind at least, a Person of Importance.

All that changed the night of the Great Fire.

It was a Thursday. Joséphine and her friend Marguerite were celebrating their third anniversary that day, and Marguerite had promised to cook a special cassoulet to mark the occasion. Joséphine couldn't wait to get home: at five to six she was busily tidying her desk and checking her handbag for the small gift she had purchased in her lunch hour. Unfortunately for her plans, she had forgotten about JoJo.

89

JoJo and his pizza van were regular and very welcome Thursday visitors to Morbignan. Connoisseurs of the delicacy claimed his bases were the lightest, his Margaritas and *Fruits de Mer* the most succulent of any pizza to be had in the area. The ladies, from giggling teenagers to sedate matrons, were won over by the twinkle in his dark eyes, the suggestive grin lurking beneath his luxuriant moustache. The moustache, JoJo reckoned, sold just as many pizzas as his culinary skills.

On the fateful Thursday, Joséphine was just about to leave when JoJo put his head round the door.

'*Merde*!' thought Joséphine, plastering on a smile, and reached for the microphone.

'*Allo! Allo*!' she gabbled. '*Le camion de pizza JoJo est installé sur la place…*' In her haste, she had knocked over the cup of coffee on her desk. It only held a few cold dregs, though, and Joséphine reckoned it could wait till morning. She had more important things to think about than a small coffee spill.

At two o'clock the following morning, a giant digger trundled through Morbignan on its way to a construction site north of the village. Its steel treads made short if noisy work of the speed bumps, and the nearby houses shivered in sympathy.

In the *mairie*, the little coffee puddle on Joséphine's desk awoke and stretched. It crept along the vibrating desk and curled itself around the microphone switch; finding a tiny gap, it began to explore downwards.

It wasn't the banging on the front door that woke Jeannette, but Useless, who landed on the bed in an urgent, barking heap, frantically paddling with her paws at her sleeping family.

'Useless? What on earth's the matter?' Jeannette peered at the alarm clock. 'It's four in the morning, for heaven's sake.'

'Mmmf? Wossit?' Henry was making a valiant effort to seem awake.

Useless stopped barking long enough for them to hear the insistent knocking below. Jeannette stumbled downstairs, wincing as her bare feet met the stone-flagged kitchen floor. She opened the front door to find Alice, in pyjamas and dressing gown, her hair standing on end.

'Fire!' said Alice breathlessly. 'There's fire in the village. Listen.'

Henry appeared at Jeannette's shoulder.

'Whaat…?'

Both women shushed him. All three listened to the hissing crackle: the fire was somewhere close.

'We have to call the *pompiers forestiers*,' said Jeannette. Forest fires were a serious threat at that time of year. After a scorching summer, when the earth was tinder-dry and the *vendange* was over, piles of *souches*, vine stumps, and the thinner, whippy *sarments* stood at the fields' edges. Soon the villagers would come to help themselves to this flammable bounty for their late barbecues and the aromatic log fires to come.

Two years earlier, Jeannette and Henry had driven out to dinner with some friends in the hills above Morbignan, only to be driven back as flames swept from tree to tree across the road.

The firemen didn't hang about. Within minutes they were racing up the main street in their huge, scarlet four-by-four Renault truck, swerving into *the rue de l'église* with a roar that banished sleep. The fire engine had hardly stopped before half a dozen firemen leapt out, braced for the onslaught.

There was nothing. Jeannot, the boss, stood foursquare in his yellow waterproofs, his thumbs hooked in the braces that held up his heavy trousers. He listened intently. Sure enough, the hiss and crackle of the flames could be heard, but where was the smell? No scent of wood smoke drifted through the streets, deliciously reminiscent of summer barbecues, but with deadly implications in the early hours of the morning

The *pompiers* were diligent. They searched the narrow streets, they sniffed attentively, they paused to listen, trying to gauge the location of the fire. There was nothing. After an hour the firemen gave up; they climbed back into the fire truck and roared off into the dawning day. Sleepers disturbed for the third time that night threw open their shutters and hurled oaths at the departing vehicle.

Morbignan woke to the sounds of a fire where no fire was to be seen. Gaston LeBlanc heard it, firing up his ovens for the morning round of baking. Matthieu, out on an emergency call, and Didier, on his way to the vines, heard the sizzle and pop. Jules et Jim, in the hills above the village, heard it faintly above the bleating of their goats.

Joséphine, arriving from home, stepped out of her Renault Clio and paused in shock. Fire! Had someone called the *pompiers?* Fumbling with the heavy iron key, she unlocked the door of the mairie. The hiss was even louder in her office: it came from the microphone. *Merde!* She must have left it switched on in her haste to leave yesterday evening. Scarlet-faced, she reached for the switch, but no: it was safely closed.

M. Pardieu arrived in a hurry.

'What's going on?' he barked.

'I don't know, *Monsieur le Maire*. I was afraid I might have left the microphone on last night…' Seeing his frown, she went on hastily, 'but I didn't. Look.'

The mayor peered at the offending mike. He tutted, he said 'Aha' several times in a knowing manner. He stuck his head out of the mairie door. Sure enough, the static from the microphone was being faithfully broadcast by the loudspeakers on the church and the *cave cooperative.*

'It's nothing,' he called to the little group who had gathered outside the *mairie.* 'Just a technical hitch. We are dealing with it.

'Joséphine,' he added, going back inside, 'get on to Languedoc Audio and have them come here *tout de suite.* They installed the system, and they can fix it.'

François arrived red-faced and apologetic. How could anything have gone wrong, he blustered. He had personally seen to the wiring, the installation of the loudspeakers and the connection of the microphone.

Armed with a voltmeter and wiring pliers he investigated the mike, tapping here, testing there. Muttering wisely to himself, he prised off the top of Joséphine's desk, emerging with a triumphant 'Aha!'

'There!' he said. 'There's your culprit. Nothing to do with me, just as I told you.'

In the cavern that had been Joséphine's desk, the formerly neat coil of wiring was a half-burnt, sticky mass.

'Something must have dripped down through that crack by the mike,' François explained. 'It would eventually have shorted out the wiring. Who spilled coffee on the desk?'

All eyes turned to the mayor's secretary.

It was a chastened Joséphine who crept through the village during the following weeks. The aura of self-importance was gone, her chin was firmly tucked into her collar and she avoided eye-contact with the grinning villagers. She went without her lunchtime *petit blanc,* knowing that if she ventured into *L'Estaminet* some wag would be sure to cry '*Au feu!* 'and take out his mobile phone in a pantomime of calling the fire brigade.

Joséphine continued to be the voice of *Allo! Allo!*, carrying out her duties efficiently and conscientiously as she had always done. She treated the butcher, the baker, the greengrocer and even JoJo himself with her usual dignified courtesy, proclaiming their wares in measured tones.

But she never ate another pizza.

Tabac or Not Tabac

'That shop's still empty, you know.' Back in Morbignan for the late-summer holiday, Henry Prendergast had been taking his traditional tour of the village.

'What shop?' Jeannette was trying to cram her groceries into Gaston's less than capacious kitchen fridge. Useless was helping, with her nose in the pâté. Henry gently hooked her back with his foot and distracted her with a biscuit.

'Kiki's shop. The *tabac*. It must be nearly a year since he disappeared.'

'He didn't disappear, Henry, don't be so melodramatic. He's living in Cap d'Agde with his new girlfriend. I think he's made it up with his kids: Mme Pardieu was saying in the *boulangerie* that Louisette went to see him on Sunday. Anyway, I'm sure we'll get a new *tabac* sooner or later.'

'Don't be so sure,' said Henry. 'I was talking to Davide…'

'Oh yes? And where was that then? Where were you talking to Davide while I was out getting the shopping?'

Henry had the grace to look sheepish. 'Yes, well I just popped into *L'Estaminet* on my way round. They were all on the terrace and Davide waved at me. It would have been rude not to.'

'Of course it would, dear,' soothed Jeannette. 'So what did Davide have to say about it?'

'Well, it seems you have to have a licence to run a *tabac*, but it's the owner that is licensed, not the premises. If Kiki hasn't passed it on, the shop can't be a *tabac* any longer.'

'That won't be much of a loss to the community. Kiki hardly sold cigarettes any more: he made most of his money selling tripperjunk to the tourists.'

'I know one person who won't be happy,' said Henry thoughtfully. 'P'tit Gui. Kiki stocked Gauloises especially for him, no-one else smoked them. Now he'll have to get in his van and go to that weird *tabac* in Les Herbes – and you never know when it is going to be open.'

It was true: the few remaining smokers in the village had long since switched to Marlborough or Benson & Hedges. Only P'tit Gui clung

94

fiercely to his Gauloises; the pungent aroma of Turkish tobacco preceded him whenever he dropped into the café for a mid-morning coffee or a pre-dinner drink.

The summer slipped into autumn; the *école primaire* opened its doors to a new batch of reluctant five-year-olds; equally reluctant, Henry and Jeannette bade farewell to Gaston and took Useless home to resume her London life. And still the *tabac* remained closed.

It was Alice who had the news. 'It's going to be a spa,' she announced, making a beeline for the corner table where Jim and Mélodie were already ensconced.

'Brr! It's cold,' she added, blowing on her fingers and looking hopefully at the carafe of red wine on the table.

Her brother and sister-in-law looked at her warily. Alice always had the news; whether it was reliable or not was moot.

'What is "it" and what is a "spa"?' Mélodie wanted to know.

'*Un salon de beauté*,' Jim translated for her. 'She's talking about Kiki's.' They both burst out laughing.

'In Morbignan?' Honestly, Alice, what will you dream of next?'

A year or two previously, an ambitious *coiffeuse* from Paris had retired to Morbignan and set up a *salon* to eke out her pension. It was not a success. The ladies of the village clung to their old ways: tightly permed heads in steel grey or the eye-watering auburn universally referred to as menopause red.

They visited tried and trusted stylists in St Rémy or Saint Laurent, disdaining the flowing tresses and subtle colours featured on posters in the window of the new establishment. Madame Fifi's, as it was derisively nicknamed, closed within ten months.

'No, it's true, Mélodie.' Alice insisted. 'You know there were people in there the other day; you told me you saw them. Well, I saw Matthieu coming out with Pierrot, that spotty apprentice of his, so I asked him. He says it's going to be a spa. He was in there doing some plumbing for the saunas.'

Mélodie had her doubts, but she said nothing more.

Another person who was saying nothing was Simon. When talk turned to the future of the *tabac* he sat back and twinkled. If he chose to, he could... said his quiet smile, but he wouldn't be drawn. The plot thickened mightily the evening Joséphine bustled importantly into the café and announced:

'Zizi's been in to see *Monsieur le Maire.*'

Joséphine was the secretary at the *mairie* – as a know-it-all when it came to village events, she gave even Alice a run for her money. A collective 'Aahhh' came from the assembled villagers. Significant looks were exchanged: if Zizi was in the picture, then Simon's reticence began to make sense. They leaned forward to hear more.

'I don't know exactly what they were talking about,' Joséphine continued, 'but Zizi had a great stack of papers and I did hear them mention a *parabole.*'

'Is that all?' said Jim. 'So she's getting a satellite dish. We've all got one.'

Joséphine's chubby features contrived to look both smug and mysterious. 'Aha, but this is a *two-metre* dish! Now what would she want with a two-metre dish, I ask you? I imagine that's what she was talking to M. Pardieu about – you can't put up something that size without a *permis*. Anyway, who knows where she's planning to put it?'

The topic languished. Getting a permit, as everyone knew, was a matter of weeks if not months. Nobody expected to hear further news of the *tabac* any time soon. Then a little Renault van from Languedoc Audio drew up one Friday morning, blocking the narrow *rue de l'église* for an hour while François, the owner, and his assistant Jean-Pierre manhandled a huge satellite dish up on to the roof of the *tabac* with the aid of many ropes and much swearing.

Job done, they stopped off for a swift *demi* in the café. Never had they been so popular. Never had so many drinks been offered them. Alas for the locals' curiosity, they had nothing to tell. 'Madame Robinson bought and paid for the *parabole* last week and asked us to install it. That's all we know.'

Simon and Zizi were suspiciously quiet. The *tabac* remained dark.

The Christmas lights went up in Morbignan. Every lamp post had its shooting star or dove of peace, the walls of *L'Estaminet* were draped in tinsel strings and a tall spruce sparkled red and green and blue and yellow in the village square. And, in the *rue de l'église*, the old *tabac* was transformed. Light spilled out into the narrow street and a wide banner in the window trumpeted the news:

"A Café for Our Times! Grand Opening January 3rd!"

Shock and consternation reigned in *L'Estaminet*. Another café in Morbignan? Unthinkable! And what was all that about a café "for our times"? The older residents whispered in corners and shook their heads. Marie Claire served her regulars tight-lipped. When Simon sauntered in with his usual cheery grin, she blanked him. Everyone knew this was all Zizi's doing.

Simon's new wife was tolerated in the village, but they didn't warm to her. When his first wife, Grace, had died, the good folk of Morbignan had rallied round the devastated widower. When, some fourteen months later, Simon returned from a trip to Paris with Zizi in tow, they were less than impressed. She was French, that was a point in her favour, but she was a *Parisienne*, which made her worse than a foreigner.

Worst of all, she was modern. When hemlines flapped respectably below the knee, Zizi flaunted her pretty legs in miniskirts. When the more daring ladies took to driving Peugeot 203s, Zizi was to be seen in a sporty little red MGB. When Simon and Zizi threw an *apéro*, a drinks party, it was more likely to be margaritas or Campari and tonic on offer than a serviceable *Picpoul de Pinet*.

But this was the final straw. If rumour were to be believed, the *Café de Nos Jours* was not just a rival for the much-loved *L'Estaminet*: it was going to be an Internet café.

Now, it's not as if the 21st Century had passed Morbignan by. The inhabitants knew about the Internet. Their children and grandchildren coaxed, threatened and cajoled them with it. 'But Papa, if you had email we could exchange news so much quicker – a letter to Paris takes forever!'

And, one by one, the villagers had conceded. They visited Darty, the electrical goods supplier, and bought computers. Email was, after all, a practical solution to keeping in touch with far-flung offspring. But that was about as far as it went.

The Internet itself was a foreign country; social media were the devil's work. Shop "online"? Do your banking *(mon dieu!)* "online"? Facebook? Twitter... No, it was all too much. Their identities would be stolen instantly if they set foot in those waters. They would be pursued through the ether by rabid trolls.

There was a moment when things might have been different, when the jewelled world of the Web might have unrolled itself at the feet of Morbignan like a magic carpet.

Allo! Allo! had announced it. The populace was invited to the *Salle des Fêtes* to discuss something called *haut débit*. Refreshments would be served. Never averse to an evening's free entertainment, not to mention a free glass or two, the Morbignanais had duly assembled.

Once the civilities and the exchange of news had died down and they had settled into their hard wooden chairs, a resplendent moustache climbed the three steps to the podium and cleared its throat. Pausing briefly to allow the populace to admire the startling growth on his upper lip, the man from the PTT (telephone company) began.

'*Mes chers amis…*'

This was ominous. When someone addressed you as a dear friend, you could be sure he was trying to sell you something. Arms folded, the audience sat back grimly, waiting to be unimpressed.

Broadband, said the man from the PTT, was coming to the village! The telephone company were planning to lay fibre cables throughout the area, and every household could be connected.

'Think of it!' he cajoled. 'You could shop, and have your shopping delivered to your door! You could find out what time the film starts without leaving your armchair! You could send pictures and documents along with your emails without waiting half an hour for them to upload! Why, you could even watch television on your computers!' The spittle flew from his lips as he extolled the wonders of this brave new world.

A murmur spread through the hall. Arms were uncrossed and people leaned forward. Tell us more, said their eager faces, tell us more. Of course, said the PTT man., returning to earth, there was the question of cost…

Ahhh. They all knew there was a catch.

'Laying cable is expensive,' explained the persuader. 'Of course, we are bringing the cable to the village at no cost to you. This is a service which France is glad to provide for the benefit of its citizens.'

The audience waited in silence.

'But connecting individual homes to the network naturally incurs additional expense. We do not feel it would be fair to lay this burden upon all residents, whether they choose to benefit or not; however, as a special one-time offer for our cherished clientele, we are prepared to connect each household for a special price of...'

He named a sum so eye-watering that there was a collective indrawing of breath, followed by a collective scuffle as the audience gathered up coats and baskets and handbags and prepared to leave the *Salle des Fêtes*. Without a word being exchanged the matter was conclusively decided: Morbignan could live without broadband.

And so it was, and so it remained – until Zizi came along. It was Jim who joined the dots. Spotting François from Languedoc Audio in the café, Jim bought him a *demi* and began to probe. It soon emerged that the massive *parabole* on the roof of the former *tabac* served one purpose: to bring broadband into Morbignan via satellite and drag the reluctant villagers out of the dark ages.

Zizi's grand opening was a triumph. The whole village turned out to drink her champagne – it was actually a rather mediocre *clairette* – admire the streamlined bar with its hanging racks of shining glasses; bottom-test the consistency of the banquette cushions and, surreptitiously, gaze into the little alcove where stood two state-of-the art computers, each with its webcam and wi-fi mouse.

Alas, in the days that followed, *Le Café de Nos Jours* stood empty. No vine-dusty elbows leaned on the bar. No coffee hissed from the sparkling Espresso machine. No babble of voices enlivened the air, and not one key of the shiny new computers was touched. Beside themselves with glee and *schadenfreude,* the regulars gathered in *L'Estaminet* to mock. Marie Claire was all smiles. Zizi's new café was going to be a disaster.

Everyone agreed that if it hadn't been for Davide's baby, Zizi would have slunk off with her pert little tail between her legs. But then there was Davide's baby...

The octogenarian former *maire* of Morbignan was, of course, way past the age of begetting babies. It was Jolie, the Brittany, who now garnered his clucks and cuddles. Even his granddaughter Mathilde was grown up now: a pretty, flirty twenty-something with teasing black eyes and a swing to her rump. And a Canadian husband.

Joel was a visiting software engineer from Toronto. As luck would have it, he had been called in to set up Zizi's computers and perform the esoteric rites that would connect them to the world wide web. Mathilde had caught his eye as she was sampling tomatoes in the market and, in an almost indecently short space of time, they were going out, engaged and then married.

All too soon, Joel's thoughts began to turn homeward. Scooping up a now-pregnant Mathilde he set off for Montpellier and thence, via Air France, to Toronto. Before they left, Joel had taken Davide to one side. A long and earnest conversation ensued which, try as they might, the patrons of *L'Estaminet* were unable to overhear. At the end of twenty minutes Davide, who had been looking sceptical, stood up with a broad grin and energetically pumped his grandson-in-law's hand.

The substance of that conversation only became clear some four and a half months later. Davide rolled into the café, delight radiating from him like a halo, and ordered drinks all round.

'I have a great-grandson!' he announced. 'He was born yesterday, weighed two and a half kilos, and he's absolutely gorgeous! Got a good pair of lungs on him, too: bawls like a sergeant major.'

'Mathilde has phoned, then?' enquired Alice. 'Has she got out of hospital already?'

'No, she's still in hospital, though they'll be going home later today. I was talking to her on Skype and...'

'What's Skype?' interrupted Alice, at the same time as Jim said:

'On the *Internet*?' and Joséphine said:

'I knew it! I thought I saw you slinking in there!' and 'Marie Claire said:

'Oh, Davide, you *didn't*!'

'Well, why not?' said the ex-*maire* grandly. 'It's not so difficult. Joel explained it all to me before they left. It's wonderful what technology can do these days. And the amazing thing is, it's free! Well, almost: Zizi charges 8€ for an hour on the computer, but that's nothing compared to the cost of a phone call.'

Marie Claire looked thoughtful. She hadn't spoken to her sister in Melbourne for more than a year. She walked over to the corner table where Simon and Zizi sat alone, sipping a pastis.

'*Salut, Zizi. Simon, ça va?*' said the café owner. 'Let me buy you a drink.'

Blackie

Elinore bustled round the kitchen in her blue quilted housecoat. She took butter, honey and *Bonne Maman* blackcurrant jam from the fridge and switched on the coffee machine. The wall calendar caught her eye and her heart fluttered with excitement. Slowly, relishing the moment, she lifted it off its hook and turned the page. October became November. Elinore couldn't contain a 'Yesss!' of triumph.

'Yes what?' Max appeared in the kitchen bearing a *baguette* and two *pains au chocolat*.

'It's November!' said Elinore gleefully. Then, seeing his blank expression, she added: 'Home time!'

Their year's stay in Morbignan la Crèbe was almost over. Max's project was complete: a state-of-the-art MRI scanner had been successfully installed in Montpellier's university hospital and it was time for them to return to Michigan.

'I can't wait!' Elinore was hopping from foot to foot. 'Just think: decent coffee, proper shopping malls. No more French. No more freaking vines. Back to civilisation!'

'Don't let the neighbours hear you say that.' Max frowned, although privately he agreed with her.

'Pooh! What neighbours? Martha and Richard are English – that's almost the same as us – and old Madame Bernières is deaf as a post and wouldn't understand even if she could hear.'

Elinore spent the next few days cleaning and packing up; Max helped by pointing out what she'd missed. They paid a last visit to the Saturday Club, where their imminent departure was greeted with polite indifference, and attended a small *apéro* party given in their honour by Max's colleagues.

Only one problem remained.

'What are we going to do about Blackie?' Martha wanted to know. The large and ill-tempered rabbit had entered their lives when they agreed to rent the house in Morbignan. Indeed, Bugs, as he was then called, was a deal-breaker: Jean Legros was off to Paris and he couldn't take the

101

creature with him, he explained. Elinore didn't blame him: was there a note of relief in his voice when he explained that Bugs was part of the fixtures and fittings?

Still, they couldn't very well abandon him, and they certainly couldn't take him back to the States with them – Elinore shuddered at the thought.

Then Max had a brainwave.

'The Pattersons, of course! They've got lots of animals, surely they won't mind one more.'

Elinore was not so sure, but it was a solution of sorts.

Martha Patterson had invited them to dinner the evening before they were due to leave. 'You'll be all packed up and you won't want to cook,' she said, 'I know how it is just before a journey.'

She was busy in the kitchen when the doorbell rang.

'I'll get it,' said Richard. He opened the door to find Max on the doorstep, his wide shoulders almost filling the door frame. Behind him stood Elinore, clutching a large cage in which crouched an enormous white rabbit with an evil glint in its eye.

'Evening,' said Max, brushing past Richard and stepping into the kitchen.

'We wondered if you wouldn't mind looking after Blackie,' said Elinore, following him in. 'We sort of inherited him from Monsieur Legros when we rented the house, but we can't take him back to America with us.'

'Er, I'm not sure…'Martha began, but Max cut in.

'Anyway, you've got lots of animals, so one more won't make a difference, will it?' Max attempted an ingratiating smile.

Martha looked at the animal with something akin to horror. 'Did you say its name was Blackie? Why…'

'Because he's white! It's a joke. We call him Blackie because he's white. Geddit? Cute, huh?'

Richard seriously considered an eye roll, but a look from Martha quelled him.

'Perhaps we can take him in for a couple of days and try and find a home for him,' Martha suggested.

'Yeah, fine. Say, something smells good. What's for dinner?'

Blackie was not a hit with the resident Patterson animals. Visitor was prepared to be friendly: she trotted over to say hello, only to leap back with a yelp as the rabbit's teeth snapped shut a fraction of an inch from her nose. Bandicoot arched his back and spat at the interloper, but Banjax just fled to his usual retreat beneath the dresser and refused to come out.

'We'll just have to keep him in that cage,' Martha decided. 'We can let him out for a run in the garden when no-one's around.'

Blackie had other ideas.

Two days after his arrival in their lives, Martha returned from a trip to Intermarché to find pandemonium in the kitchen. The rabbit had made short work of the simple pin securing his cage, and now crouched in the doorway, ears flat, red eyes peering malevolently around him. Facing him was Bandicoot, the fur on his spine bristling, a low growl issuing from his throat. Banjax was seated behind his brother, licking at a trickle of red that ran down his foreleg. Visitor was dancing round the tableau, barking hysterically.

Martha grabbed Blackie firmly by the scruff of the neck, taking care to avoid his teeth and the raking claws on his hind feet. She shoved him back into the cage and tied the door securely with fuse wire.

Richard wandered in; the cacophony had penetrated even his creative haze.

'What's to do?' he enquired.

'What's to do is that rabbit has to go. I can't have my family's peace disrupted like this.'

'Fine,' said Richard. 'Let's take him up to the lake and set him free. There's hundreds of rabbits up there.'

'We can't do that. He's a domestic rabbit, the ones up there are wild. Even if they don't kill him, he won't know how to forage. He'll starve to death.'

'Good riddance,' said Richard, but he knew that his wife's soft heart would never countenance such a thing.

'How about Madame Brieux?' Martha said suddenly. The old lady lived on the edge of the village in a ramshackle cottage, surrounded by an acre or two of *garrigue*. She was known locally as the cat woman – she had thirteen – but her menagerie extended to three dogs, a dozen or so rabbits, a goat, a handful of chickens and a fierce cockerel.

'I'm sure she'll take Blackie,' Martha went on. 'She's got lots of rabbits, so one more won't make…' she clapped her hand over her mouth. Richard was laughing.

'Why, you sound just like my good ol' buddy Max,' he jeered.

Martha giggled. 'Yes, all right, I know. But the point is Madame Brieux is about the only person I know we could foist Blackie on to. And the other rabbits will soon sort him out. It'll do him good not to have it all his own way.'

Richard volunteered to do the deed. Martha was dubious: Richard's French was not exactly fluent and she wondered if he would manage.

'I've got to go over that way anyway,' he said, 'I have to see the *garagiste*. The car's been making some funny noises and I want him to have a look at it.'

Madame Brieux looked curiously at the tall Englishman on her doorstep, clutching a cage containing a large white rabbit. As best he could, Richard explained the situation. The old lady shook her head. He tried again; more head shaking. Then he had an inspiration. '*Gardiane!*' he said. '*Vous gardiane lapin!*'

She looked at him uncertainly. '*Gardiane lapin, Monsieur? Non. Pas possible.*'

'*Si, Madame, s'il vous plait*' Richard pleaded.

Madame Brieux shrugged her shoulders. '*Eh bien, Monsieur, si c'est ce que vous voulez vraiment...*'

'*Pardon, Madame?*' Richard was lost.

'Eef you want really, I say yes.'

Mission accomplished, Richard returned home in triumph. Bandicoot and Visitor were asleep by the fire, paws entwined. Banjax was ensconced in his usual lair, but he was purring drowsily. Peace reigned.

A loud knock the next morning brought Martha running to the front door. Madame Brieux stood outside in the rain; in her hands was an earthenware crock. Delicious smells were issuing from the crock.

Martha hurriedly invited the old lady in and poured her a cup of coffee.

'*Pour vous*, Monsieur', said Madame Brieux, thrusting the crock at Richard, who was still dawdling over his *Midi Libre*.

'*Pour moi?*' he repeated.

'*Oui, Monsieur, pour vous. La Gardiane.*'

Martha gasped. 'Oh, dear, what did you say to her?'

''I was trying to make her understand that I'd brought Blackie to her because she is the village's animal guardian.'

'Tell me,' said Martha slowly, '*exactly* what word you used.'

104

'I said *gardiane*, of course. It's practically the same as the English word.'

'No, it isn't, dear.' Martha was trying hard not to laugh. She turned away to pour the old lady another cup of coffee. Her shoulders were shaking.

'Rick, dear, *Gardiane* is a local word for a kind of casserole, like a *daube*. Madame Brieux has turned poor old Blackie into a stew.'

Beginnings

'No, Gaston, I was never your childhood sweetheart. When I was ten you were fifteen and much too grown-up to notice me.'

The lunch-hour rush was over, and Gaston Bergerac sat in a corner of the café with the remains of his coffee. He rested his chin on his hands, clasped on the handle of his elegantly carved walking stick, and twinkled at Marie Claire.

'I remember you at school, Marcie,' he reminisced, pretending not to notice as she winced at the nickname. 'You were such a pretty little thing; all the boys were after you. But you fancied me. Yes, you know you did. I used to sit behind you and pull your pigtails and make you giggle.'

'Now you're being sentimental and silly,' she retorted. 'We were never in the same class at school, and besides, I didn't have pigtails. My hair was short: I only grew it when I went to work for Babette. She liked to practise styles on me when the salon wasn't busy. Anyway, you only had eyes for Béatrice.'

The smile in Gaston's eyes dimmed, and Marie Claire regretted bringing up the name of his late wife. It had been a love match, the talk of their teenage years. At the Lycée Paul Riquet in St Rémy, the youngsters had been about to go into *seconde* – the year when life for the pupils became serious as they started to prepare for the *Baccalauréat*. Béatrice had walked into the classroom on the first day of the school year. The students, who had all known each other virtually from the cradle, turned as one to scrutinise this new face. The boys sat up straighter, the girls checked their hair. Béatrice was a beauty.

At break time the newcomer stood shyly apart, until a group of girls clustered round her with questions: where had she come from? Why had she come to St Rémy? Where did she buy that jacket?

At the opposite end of the recreation yard the boys were exchanging boasts. Each one of them saw himself strutting into the next school disco with the pretty new girl on his arm. Only Gaston was silent. The moment he had seen her, his stomach had clenched and his mouth had gone dry.

'This,' said a little voice inside him, 'this is the girl I shall marry.'

106

It wasn't love at first sight. Béatrice was a Parisienne: she had moved to St Rémy with her parents when her father inherited a small vineyard and decided to swap his desk and formal suit for dungarees and secateurs.

At her fashionable Lycée in the *quatrième arrondissement* Béatrice had had her pick of escorts: her most recent boyfriend was an alluring eighteen-year-old with a motor bike and a burgeoning moustache. Her mother fretted that the young man was altogether too fascinating for her not-quite-sixteen-year-old daughter; she welcomed the move to a more rural location, despite the tantrums the prospect provoked.

Casting her eyes over the preening boys, Béatrice decided that her immediate future held nothing but celibacy. She would, she vowed, concentrate on her studies, take honours in her exams and pursue an adventurous career at the Sorbonne, far from watchful parental eyes. It was a few days before she noticed Gaston. He was different from the others: quieter, but more intense. When his eyes met hers she felt an unsettling flutter in the pit of her stomach.

'I wonder,' she said to herself. 'I wonder.'

As the end of term approached, and with it the traditional discotheque, Gaston made his move.

'Béatrice, would you care to come to the dance with me?' The formal speech disguised his nervousness.

Béatrice smiled and the matter was settled: from that moment on they were boyfriend and girlfriend and, soon after graduating, husband and wife. It was a happy marriage, but not a very long one. Five years after Jeannette, their youngest, was born, Béatrice began to suffer the symptoms of the cancer that would eventually kill her.

For three years Gaston had been inconsolable. As Jeannette grew up and went as a *pensionnaire* (boarder) to the Lycée in St Rémy, he settled into a fierce and lonely routine: breakfast on his little terrace, an hour or two sitting silent in the square while his cronies chattered and tried to engage him in conversation.

On Fridays he would take lunch at the café, deriving some small comfort from the gentle concern of the owner, Marie Claire. She never pushed him, but if he wanted to talk, she would listen. Eighteen years passed. Gaston began to take an interest in life again, but the sadness remained.

Today in the café, Marie Claire watched the play of joy and pain on Gaston's face as, his eyes lost in memory, he relived the good and bad times.

'Gaston?' she said, bringing him back to the present.

'Ah yes, where were we?' the twinkle had returned. 'Well, childhood sweetheart or not, I have a very important question to ask you.

'Madame, would you do me the honour of accompanying me to the ball?'

Marie Claire breathed a sigh of relief. For a moment she had been afraid that the "important question" might be something more serious than an invitation to accompany him to the Bastille Day festivities. He had, after all, been paying her an increasing amount of attention lately.

'*Je serais enchantée*,' she agreed with a smile.

Gaston's daughter Jeannette and Henry, her English husband, would be over for *Le Quatorze*. Usually they visited her father in September, but this year Jeannette had insisted they be in France for the celebrations.

'It might not be so convenient for me to travel in September,' she said mysteriously.

As IQs went, Henry's was definitely in the upper bracket. He had done the Mensa tests and been accepted, then resigned from the club because he found his fellow members boring. But, when all was said and done, he was only a man. Feminine innuendo was beyond his grasp.

'Why? What's happening in September?' he wanted to know. 'Can't you get leave? They know you always go on holiday in September…'

Henry stopped, aware that Jeannette was looking at him meaningfully. He hated it when she looked at him meaningfully: it made him feel stupid. Then the penny dropped.

'You mean…' he said. It was the worst kind of cliché, and he knew it.

'Yup. You're going to be a *papa* after all.'

They had been trying half-heartedly for a while. Jeannette was ambivalent about babies. They were all very well when other people had them, but she wasn't at all sure she wanted one of her own. She adored her job as assistant editor of a fashion magazine, not least because the editor was indulgent when it came to time off.

If Jeannette wanted a few days in France she could usually persuade her boss to count it as research; Jeannette had a sharp eye for the latest trends in Paris fashion and more than once had come back with a photo feature that left other magazines in the shade.

Lately, however, she had begun to wonder if, perhaps, she did want to be a mother after all.

Henry was overjoyed. He had no doubts: parenthood was exactly what he wanted, but a question fizzed in his brain.

'How on earth are we going to tell Useless?' he asked. 'She's been used to being an only dog, what will she think of a new arrival?'

'*Artemis*' said Jeannette pointedly, 'will have to cope. She loves other dogs, people and puppies. We'll just tell her that this is our puppy.'

June slipped into July. Bunting appeared in the streets, and tricolours sprouted from balconies and flower tubs. Morbignan was getting into festive mood. Gaston, on the other hand, was pensive. He had a decision to make. Marie Claire was surprised to see him in the café at lunchtime one Wednesday, not his usual day at all.

'What's the matter, *mon chou*, have you forgotten how to cook?' she teased him. Gaston just shook his head; his face was sombre. The following morning he was spotted at the bus stop at 8:30, waiting for the bus to St Rémy. This was juicy enough for the gossips to get their teeth into; they would have been astounded had they seen Gaston cross the little square of the terminus in St Rémy and board the bus to Montpellier.

Jeannette and Henry arrived on the afternoon of the 13th. As usual there was pandemonium: shouts of greeting, hugs and kisses from the humans while Gaston's dog Maître hurled himself ecstatically at Useless in a cacophony of barks and yelps.

When peace was restored and they were settled on the shady terrace with a glass of wine, Jeannette shared her news. Gaston made all the right noises, asked all the right questions, but Jeannette detected an unexpected note of reserve.

'What's the matter, *papa*, aren't you pleased?' she asked anxiously.

'Of course I am, *chérie*. I'm delighted. My first English grandchild! That'll be one in the eye for Monique, she's always bragging about her family in Paris. I can't wait to tell her…'

'But?' Jeannette prompted. She knew her father, and something was troubling him.

'Nothing, nothing at all, *chouchou,* only I may have some news of my own before long.'

109

Tease him though they might, Jeannette and Henry could get nothing more out of Gaston. He sat smiling enigmatically until they gave up; he would tell them in his own good time.

At the supper in the village square the next night, Gaston and his family were joined by Marie Claire. Jeannette was delighted to see her – she had always treated the café owner as a mother and Marie Claire, childless herself, had developed a great fondness for her.

'Marie Claire, we'll be in the café for lunch tomorrow and we'll expect one of your wonderful *daubes*,' said Jeannette.

The meal was ending when a hiss, a crackle and a cascade of blue and white stars announced the traditional July 14 fireworks. Stumbling and laughing in the dark, the villagers made their way down the stony track to the field where the display was being staged.

Twenty minutes later, as the last spurt of red, white and blue faded against the deeper blue of the sky, the strains of an accordion drifted down from the *place*. Soon the dancing would begin.

Tucking Marie Claire's hand beneath his arm, Gaston led her aside.

'Marie Claire…' he paused, uncertain how to go on. Fumbling in his pocket he brought out a small, square box. It was dark red leather tooled in gold, and stamped on its lid was the logo of a very expensive jeweller in Montpellier.

'Marie Claire, will you?'

'Will I what?' she teased. He looked so stricken that she relented. 'Will I marry you, is that it? Well…'

'Say yes, please do, Marie Claire. You know I've come to love you…'

'Love my cooking more like!'

'No, I mean it. I love you and I want to spend the rest of my life with you. And I know you love children: if you marry me, you'll have four, plus seven – no, nearly eight grandchildren…'

Marie Claire hid her face in her hands; her shoulders were shaking. Horrified, Gaston put his arm round her, cuddling her close.

'Don't cry, *chérie,* I didn't mean to upset you.'

When Marie Claire raised her head there were tears of laughter on her cheeks.

'Marry you for your grandchildren?' she gasped. 'That's the weirdest proposal I've ever heard of. You'll be telling me next that Maître needs a mother!'

'So it's "no", then?' Gaston was crestfallen.

'No. It's not "no", you silly goose. Of course I will marry you. But I have one condition. I won't live in that draughty old house of yours. It's too inconvenient and there are too many stairs. There's plenty of room in my bungalow and it's got both central heating and *clim'*, air conditioning, for when it gets really hot.'

'But what about Maître?'

'What *about* Maître? I have always welcomed him into my café, so why wouldn't I welcome him into my home?'

Jeannette looked at her father in astonishment when he broke the news. 'You're getting married?'

'Yes, why? Don't you approve?

'Of course I approve, it's the most wonderful thing I've heard in ages. I've always loved Marie Claire, and she'll be good for you. She doesn't take you too seriously – and she's a good cook too!'

'There is just one problem,' Gaston looked thoughtful. 'Marie Claire doesn't want to live in my house so I am going to move in with her. I'll have to sell the house, though, and there won't be room for you all when you come to visit.'

'Don't worry about us,' Henry butted in. 'There are plenty of *gites* and apartments in St Rémy, and probably some in Morbignan if we ask around. If you think you're getting out of seeing us every year you've got another think coming.'

But later that night, alone with Jennette, Henry had a plan.

'How about if we bought your father's house? There's plenty of room for us, and Use – I mean Artemis – and the baby, and any more babies that may come along, too. I know the kitchen is a bit old-fashioned, but we can soon put in some improvements.

'How about it, Jeannette? You love the house, you love the village and you love seeing *papa* and Marie Claire.'

Jeannette was almost speechless. 'Could we really do that? I've always dreamed of having a house here, but I never thought it would really happen.'

'We'll make it happen,' said Henry firmly. 'And just think, we'll be able to come over whenever we feel like it, without worrying about disturbing your father. We can come at Christmas, and Easter too if you want, as well as the summer.'

Jeannette's eyes were shining. 'Just think of it, Henry. Won't it be wonderful? A real family home in the Pays d'Oc!'

the end

AFTERWORD

From the collected works of Richard Patterson

I

The Sad Ballade of the Indian Prawn

There was a diner and he loved his food
Sing hey nonny, nonny, nonny no.
There was a thief who was up to no good
Singing hey nonny, hey nonny no.

Said the diner one day to his wife dear and true:
'I fancy an Indian supper, do you?
I've a tandoori craving for chicken and spice
So if you'd call the take-away, that would be nice.'

So his wife, all obedient, called the Monsoon
And said to them 'Please bring our dinner quite soon.
Mixed grill for my husband, Passanda for me,
With rice and parathas and an onion bhaji.'

And soon the meal came, with aromas delish.
There was chicken and keema kebab on his dish
And - the thing that the diner loved most in his life
(Second only of course to his dog and his wife) -

To his beaming delight in the tandoori there sat a
Succulent prawn in the midst of the platter.
Said the diner 'I'm saving this morsel for last:
It's just what I like to conclude the repast.'

But did he but know it, a thief was about:
A four-footed felon with burglarious snout.

She lovingly snuffed up the smell of the food:
For tandoori grill she was just in the mood.

Her master ate quickly, 'twas almost too late,
And she didn't once take her brown eyes off his plate.
Then a scheme popped up into the ne'er do well's head:
With a shriek she leapt up, to the back door she fled.

She barked and she barked. Such a noise did she make
That the man left his dinner – a foolish mistake.
He hurried to open the garden door wide
So the vigilant dog could patrol the outside.

But cunning, oh cunning, the dog rushed about
And back through his legs she returned. With a shout
Of terror and anguish the man saw his prawn
But just for an instant, and then it had gorn!

For tripping on tiptoes the felon did snare
The prawn from the plate that the diner left there
And fled from the kitchen, a smile in her eyes
And proceeded to munch on her ill-gotten prize.

A moral there is to this tale I relate:
Never leave unattended the meal on your plate.
No matter how loudly you hear the dog bawl
Keep your eye on your prawn or you'll lose it – that's all.

So if you're a diner and you like your food
Sing hey nonny nonny nonny no
Beware of the thief who is up to no good
Singing hey nonny hey nonny no.

A-sitting on a Bench

I'll tell thee everything I can
Concerning matters French,
And of an aged, aged man
A-sitting on a bench.

'Who are you, aged man?' I cried,
'And tell me why you sit
Upon a bench in Morbignan.
Pray, what's the sense in it?'

He said 'I'm old, as you can see
My days of toil are done.
And so I'm here upon my bench
A-sitting in the sun.'

Just then another four came up
And stood beside the first.
And cried 'The café beckons us
For we've an awful thirst.

'And if you care to stand us, sir,
A *rouge*, or a *demi*
We'll gladly tell to you our tale
For ancient men are we.

And we have laboured in the fields
And tended of the vine
And so to rest upon our bench
We think it right and fine.'

I took those ancient, ancient men
Across the road to drink.
But, sadly, when they'd drunk their fill
In torpor they did sink.

And so I never heard the tale
Explaining why the French
In dotage like to pass their time
A-sitting on a bench.

MURDER

IN THE PAYS D'OC

Principal characters

more or less in order of appearance

Thierry	a retired *vigneron*
Céleste	his wife
Richard Patterson	an English poet
Martha	his wife
Ignace ('Papa') Pardieu``	mayor of Morbignan
Joséphine	his secretary
Gaspard Petit	the most hated man in the village, formerly the jewel thief Le Petit Chat
Mireille (Mimi)	his wife
Jean-Jacques Depardieu	a wealthy *vigneron,* Mimi's father
Isabelle (Ysabel)	village girl seduced by Gaspard. Later a famous writer
Bienvenue	her daughter
François Peitavy	Isabelle's father, former *notaire* of Morbignan,
Claude Laforge	Isabelle's boyfriend
Bernard Durand	a retired policeman
Lili	his wife, a famous singer
Gérard	founder of the band where Lili makes her début
Jean-Luc and Jean-Marc	identical twins, Gaspard's cousins
Sylvie de Lacoste	victim of the twins' scam. Later, soon-to-be-ex-wife of Robin Thornfield
Marquise de Saint Esprit	her aunt, victim of the twins' scam
Henry Prendergast	always known as *l'anglais*
Jeannette	his wife
James Carcenet	an English bookseller
Alex	his wife
Betty	his mother-in-law
Tiphaine	an antique dealer
Robin Thornfield	a fat Englishman

The boy and girl ran hand in hand down the stone steps behind the church. Summer visitors to Morbignan, they had escaped their respective families for a romantic stroll along the river.

At the point where the steps twisted sharply to the left stood a crumbling building, the remains of an old wash house. Weeds pushed up through the floor and the walls were encrusted with lichen.

The boy pulled the girl inside.

'Not in here, Chuck,' she protested. 'It's filthy and it smells of pee.'

'No, just for a minute. I want to show you something cool.'

There were some words scrawled on the wall in fading marker pen.

The boy read them aloud:

'Question: what is the difference between French beer and a dead frog?

Answer: there's more hops in a dead frog.'

The girl screamed.

'Aw, come on, honey,' said the boy. 'It's not such a bad joke.'

'No, look!' Her eyes were huge in her white face as she pointed. 'There's a frog out there. I think he's dead!'

The boy's gaze followed her shaking finger out through the hole where a window had been. The lower part of the steps was visible from here.

Gaspard Petit lay twisted at the bottom, his neck bent at an impossible angle. His open eyes stared up into the unseeing sky.

Chapter 1:

EXPECTATIONS OF A PARTY,
RUMOURS OF A LION

Morbignan La Crèbe, Wednesday
three days before the party

July in the little village of Morbignan la Crèbe, nestling beneath the Cévenne mountains in the heart of the Languedoc. After a couple of false starts, the hot weather has set in with a vengeance. Villagers abandon their winter quarters and seek the cool refuge of their garages, now set out as summer living rooms - *salons d'été*. The river, so turbulent in the winter rains, is just a slender trickle between dry beds of scrub and grasses. The summer visitors take their picnics to the stepping-stones, never tiring of congratulating themselves on lunching in mid-stream.

In *l'Estaminet* Marie Claire, just back from honeymoon, can hardly keep up with the orders for chilled beers and Coca Cola, and the calls for *'encore des glaçons, s'il t'plait'* ('more ice, please') keep her new daughter, Jeannette, running back and forth to the big freezer behind the kitchen. Marie Claire's new husband -- and Jeannette's father -- Gaston Bergerac has made himself comfortable in a corner of the bar and is deep in conversation with his English son-in-law Henry.

In the *Place de la République*, dogs slump in whatever shade they can find, tongues lolling above the scorching earth. Tourists depart daily in sweltering cars, laden to the teeth with deck chairs and picnic baskets, to the derision of the locals who know better. The good ol' boys in the square have at last discarded their mufflers and heavy coats and sit at ease on the circular bench under the great plane tree, coloured handkerchiefs adorning their brows.

The bunting has gone up in the village square. The *tricolore* hangs limply from the flagstaff in front of the *mairie* and the same flag adorns the windows of the *patisserie* and Lydia's little grocery shop. Behind the scenes, the ladies of the fête committee are counting chairs and assessing the merits of *traiteurs* (caterers). It is only a few days now until the grand July 14th celebration, Bastille Day.

In her cool, stone-built house overlooking the river, Céleste was plotting.

'*Bon anniversaire, chéri,*' she greeted her husband, slipping a silver-paper-wrapped box into his hand.

Thierry was not to be cajoled. He glowered at his wife.

'Bah! Happy birthday? What is there to celebrate?' he growled. 'Sixty years! How can I be 60 years old? And how many years have I got left?'

Céleste planted a kiss on his mahogany pate and went to the kitchen to make the coffee. She knew better than to broach the subject of a birthday party with her husband in this mood.

The phone beeped and she grabbed the handset before Thierry could hear and demand to know who was calling at this hour.

'*Maman?*' said her younger daughter's voice. 'Is everything ready?'

Céleste smiled. She and Zara were co-conspirators in the affair of Thierry's party.

'*Oui, chérie,* everything is ready,' she reassured her daughter.

All was, indeed, ready. Thierry's cronies had been primed. P'tit Gui the builder, Sylvestre the woodman and Kiki, on an occasional visit back to the village, would stop by next Saturday afternoon. They would, they promised, drag Thierry off to *l'Estaminet* for a celebratory drink. They would brook no resistance.

Then, while Thierry was safely ensconced in the bar, Céleste, Zara and her boyfriend Jean-Luc would make the house ready. In no time flat they would light candles, blow up balloons, hang bunting and lay out the feast prepared in secret by Dominique, the couple's elder daughter. Friends, relatives, villagers and passing dogs were all bidden to be there *à six heures pile* – six o'clock on the dot. And at six thirty (to allow for the laxity of Midi timekeeping) the gang of three would escort Thierry back to his house for the *grande surprise*.

There would, Céleste knew, be a pretence of anger, a thrusting-out of lower lip. But then Thierry's eyes would start to twinkle and soon he would be revelling in the congratulations, the presents, the *bisous*, the shoulder thumps.

An invitation (Shh!)

The following morning, Richard Patterson was looking puzzled.

'Martha, we've had a most mysterious note,' he said walking into the kitchen where his wife was making coffee. 'This has just been pushed under our door.'

He handed her a white envelope, blank except for the single word *'Chut!'* scrawled in black letters across the front.

'Here's an idea: why not open it?' Martha Patterson regarded her husband with a mixture of affection and exasperation as he fished in the kitchen drawer. Forestalling him, she removed her best kitchen knives from his reach and handed him an elderly butter knife. Carefully, he slit open the envelope and removed a scrap of paper. 'You are invited...' he read aloud slowly.

'Yes, yes, invited to *what*?'

Her husband blinked at her reproachfully. '... to Thierry's birthday party on Saturday. But it's a surprise. *Chut!* I presume that means *Shhh!* We mustn't say a word. And there's more. Céleste says there is going to be a *very special* guest of honour. I wonder...'

'It'll be the author,' Martha broke in excitedly. 'Céleste's very thick with Joséphine, who's organising the whole thing. I'll bet she has managed to get Ysabel de la Fontaine to come to the party. Of course, Thierry won't have a clue who she is, but it'll be a huge coup for Céleste. I'm so looking forward hearing Ysabel's talk tonight.'

The village was abuzz with the news. Ysabel de la Fontaine, a famous comic novelist, was coming to Morbignan for a talk and a meet-the-author session at the *Salle des Fêtes*.

Nobody really knew how this literary lion had been captured by the modest village. One day a letter appeared on the desk of 'Papa' Pardieu, the mayor, graciously accepting his invitation to come and give a talk. Try as he might, Pardieu couldn't get to the bottom of it. Who had issued the invitation? Everyone on the *fête* committee denied knowledge. Still,

126

one doesn't look a gift horse in the mouth, so he replied, thanking her for her generosity and confirming the details.

Truth be told, the villagers weren't great readers. A glance at the TV magazine or a peek into *Marie Claire* was about the height of literary ambition for most people. Still, they took a proprietorial interest in Ysabel, whose wonderfully funny novels had taken the critics and the public by storm and who, rumour insisted, had actually been born in Morbignan! No-one was going to turn down a chance to meet the famous author.

Martha Patterson had picked up a copy of *Les Aventures de Glou-glou* at the airport two weeks earlier, on a weekend trip back to the UK. She was grinning before the plane had left the runway, and by the time they landed she could hardly contain herself.

'You won't believe it, it's Gaspard!' she had crowed to her husband on her mobile.

'Hmm? What's Gaspard?' As usual, it took Richard a moment or two to catch up with his wife's exuberant exclamations

'*Les Aventures de Glou-glou*. I got a copy at the airport because I left *The Other Boleyn Girl* on my bedside table, dammit, and I had to have something to read on the plane. But you won't believe this. You know that author who's coming to give a talk at the *Salle des Fêtes* next month? Ysabel de la Fontaine, she's called. She's written a series of books about this character called *Glouglou*.

'I'd never read any of them before, but this fellow is the spit and image of Gaspard Petit. He's fat and unpleasant and, as you would put it, he definitely crawled out of the shallow end of the gene pool.

'Of course, it could be a coincidence; Ysabel is very mysterious about her origins but I heard somewhere that the she was born in Morbignan, and that she has a Past. You know what writers are like: if this Ysabel person had ever met Gaspard, well, he's absolute comedy gold isn't he? And he's extremely fond of *rosé* - I imagine that's why she calls him *Glou-glou*.'

Silence from the other end.

'Oh, honestly Rick, haven't you learned anything?' Martha huffed. '*Glou-glou* means glug-glug. As in wine?'

'Well, he'll never know about the book,' Richard Patterson said. 'I don't think he's the sort who goes in for reading.'

He was to be proved wrong.

Enter the Lion

Joséphine, the mayor's secretary, was all a-bustle. Ysabel de la Fontaine was due to arrive at Montpellier station at 12:55.

'Now someone will have to go and meet her from the train,' Joséphine ordered. 'No, not you, Jean-Luc, your Peugeot is far too cramped: remember she will have quite a bit of luggage with her.'

She looked expectantly at Gaspard Petit. His Renault Nevada estate was by far the most spacious car in the village. Gaspard grunted.

'I'll take that as a *"Oui, avec plaisir, Joséphine"* the secretary said tartly. 'Now go and get yourself cleaned up, and for goodness' sake have a shave!'

Stepping off the train at Montpellier, Ysabel swung the heavy silk shawl over her shoulder with a theatrical gesture. Close on her heels, a young woman struggled with a heavy suitcase.

Ysabel looked about her for the person who was to meet them and couldn't restrain a small cry of glee as Gaspard lurched towards her. He was older, fatter, with the tale of many dissipations etched into his bulbous nose and bloodshot eyes; yet this was unmistakably the man who had changed her life. As chauffeur to a celebrity, he left a lot to be desired. His jeans were ragged at the hem and his t-shirt, though fairly clean, bore the ghost of many a stain. On his chest was a battered enamel pin depicting a black cat sitting on a wall.

As expected, Gaspard did not offer to help Ysabel and her companion with their luggage. Instead, he gestured abruptly and turned towards the car park, leaving the two women to follow as best they could. Ysabel chuckled quietly: she had her own agenda.

'This is most kind of you, Monsieur Petit,' she purred when they reached the car. 'And I believe you have also volunteered to take me back to Montpellier station when I return to Paris. I do hope you will allow me to take you to lunch, as a small thank you.'

And to herself she murmured: 'You don't recognise me, do you, *mon chou?*' Now we'll have some fun.'

Indeed, the svelte and glamorous author bore no resemblance to the naïve village girl she had been. Her mind drifted back to those desperate months in Paris, some 20 years ago.

Chapter 2:

GASPARD AND
THE NOTAIRE'S DAUGHTER

Morbignan and Paris. 1998

Isabelle

'Bienvenue,' thought Isabelle, looking at the tiny bundle cradled in her arms. 'I shall call her Bienvenue because, in spite of everything, she is most welcome.'

Her thoughts drifted back to the previous year. It was all Claude's fault, she decided, Claude and his boring plans and his boring expectations.

To be honest, she hadn't really wanted a boyfriend. At 17, a gang of laughing friends and some serious studying took up most of her time. And writing, of course. Isabelle was going to be a famous writer. Madame Coudroy said so, and the formidable head teacher was never wrong.

It hadn't been the most auspicious of beginnings, though. The students had started a clandestine newspaper; naturally it was never meant to fall in into the teachers' hands and, naturally, it did. The culprits were soon identified and summoned to the head's study. The paper, and not least Isabelle's satirical take on the morning assembly, complete with pen portraits - of the least flattering kind - of all her teachers, had earned the editorial gang of six a month of detentions and a stern warning about applying themselves to their schoolwork.

What they didn't know was that Eveline Coudroy had had some difficulty keeping a straight face as the downcast gaggle of teenagers

130

made their way out of her office. 'She's a little firecracker,' Eveline had confided to her crony, Mademoiselle Dupuis, in the staff room later that day. 'If Isabelle Peitavy doesn't make a name for herself with her writing, I shall be very surprised.'

Isabelle and her co-conspirators, meanwhile, were enjoying an unprecedented wave of popularity following the incident, and that was when Claude Laforge stepped into the picture. Tall, athletic, with a carefully cultivated tumble of Byronesque curls and a well groomed moustache, he was the most sought-after boy in their year. Swept off her feet, Isabelle failed to realise, until it was too late, was that he was also the most boring. When she was writing, he wanted to snog. When she was working on her essay, he wanted to go to a rugby match. When she talked of a career, he scoffed.

They had been dating eight months when he proposed. It was the night of the Christmas disco, the last she would attend as a schoolgirl. Isabelle had news to share.

'It's happening!' Her eyes shone with excitement. 'I've actually got a job with *France Soir*! In Paris! Coudroy fixed it. Of course, it'll be very junior, I'll probably just be making the coffee, but it's Paris! I'll meet artists and writers and…' she tailed off. Claude was looking at her boot-faced.

'Nonsense' was all he said. To her horror, he got down on one knee, producing a small red velvet covered box.

'Isabelle, you are going to be my wife. I have known this since the moment I met you. You don't need to worry about earning a living. I am going to take care of you, so you'll never have to work. You will be a mother to our children and a wonderful asset to me in my diplomatic career, in which I intend to go far.'

'No!' Her hand shot out in denial, knocking the box from his grasp.

For a moment they both stood frozen, then she turned and ran from the school hall. At the very same moment, Gaspard Petit was slouching into the hall, eyes on the prowl for something tasty to flaunt on the pillion of his Harley, which was parked impudently next to the railings in the maths teacher's parking spot.

Isabelle had seen him around the school from time to time and taken note. He was everything that Claude was not. A bit of a scoundrel, a bit of a waster, he made his living picking up odd jobs where he could – in the vines, in the café, at *the cave coopérative*.

He also held a part-time post as school caretaker at the Lycée in St Rémy, Isabelle's school, which gave him ample opportunity to eye up pretty schoolgirls. He was a sharp dresser, and only the keenest eye could detect any signs of 'pre-loving': he bought his clothes from the *Frip'* – the second-hand clothes stall in St Rémy whose canny owner made frequent trips to Paris. And always, always the mysterious pin with the black cat on it.

He was older: his 27 years and dark good looks gave him a louche glamour in Isabelle's eyes. He was also, as Isabelle was to find out too late, engaged to be married.

That evening, Isabelle was in the mood for adventure. Speeding down the Rue de l'Eglise on the back of the Harley, she saw a world of possibilities open up before her.

In the days that followed, Isabelle was in a whirl of happiness. Claude was forgotten. True, when she outlined her plans to Gaspard, he was barely more supportive than the discarded boyfriend, but at least he didn't laugh at her ambition. Each evening, when the bell rang for the end of classes, she would dart out of school, thrilled to find him waiting for her astride his beloved motorcycle. December was mild that year, and they would ride out through the vines and up into the hills beyond, where they would sit gazing at the patchwork of vineyards and houses spreading out before them.

Eventually, of course, the inevitable happened. When Gaspard led her to the abandoned shepherd's hut and took her in his arms, she surrendered in a mixture of fear and excitement.

'I love you,' she murmured, but he only said 'Shh…'

Three months later, when she had gone to him in tears and hope with her news, he had shrugged his shoulders.

'Who's to say it's mine?' he'd jeered. 'You should have taken better care; this was only meant to be a bit of fun. You didn't think I loved you, did you? And if you tell anyone, I shall just deny it. Mimi and I are getting married soon. Her father has 1,500 hectares of vines and a nice little wine bottling business on the side. I'll be set up for life when I marry her, so why should I bother with the daughter of a small-town *notaire*?'

Unable to face her parents, Isabelle had turned to the one person she knew would help her, Madame Coudroy. The head teacher had fussed and scolded and organised.

'Well you've really messed up your life, you silly girl, haven't you?' she said. 'The best thing you can do is go and talk to your parents.'

Isabelle was adamant: *Maman* and *Papa* mustn't know: they would be so angry and disappointed in her. Madame Coudroy came up with a solution.

'I've spoken to my sister in Paris,' she told Isabelle two days later. 'You can stay with her until after the baby is born and you decide what to do. You can kiss goodbye to that job at *France Soir*, though, they won't hold it for you. You'll just have to have a good think and start again.'

'How?' she had thought bleakly. How could she start again? She was 18, she had lost the job that was going to open doors for her, she would soon be a mother. How could she provide for herself and the child and still have a life? Nevertheless, her teacher's words stayed with her.

Now, as she cradled her baby daughter, she began to have the glimmering of an idea. Bur first – she looked at her watch – there were preparations to make. There was wine to pour, *pâté en croute* to slice, salted almonds and pistachios to set out in bowls. She was expecting her friends Annette and Marie-Paulle: they were coming to meet the most-welcome baby and inspect the tiny flat Isabelle had found in the *sixième arrondissement.*

Like herself, the two women were single mothers. Isabelle had bonded with them at ante-natal clinics, regaling them with stories of her past – the stodgy boyfriend, the undesirable lover - and always with the comic twist that was becoming her trademark. 'Stop,' they entreated her, tears running down their faces. 'Stop, or we'll be wetting our *culottes* (knickers) as well as our cheeks.'

The evening was a success. They had brought their babies with them, and also Farouk, their friend, birthing partner and devoted slave.

'You'll love Farouk,' they had assured her. 'He's very… different.'

'*Enchanté mademoiselle,*' he had murmured, shrugging off his sage green velvet cloak and bending low over her hand so that his exuberant moustache tickled her fingers.

'Tell Farouk the stories about Claude,' her friends begged her, and soon the four adults were howling with laughter as the babies slept.

'Mademoiselle, you are a genius,' Farouk declared as they left. 'You are a born *raconteuse* and, I suspect, an author in the making. I beseech you, set these stories down and you will have a *succès de foudre*. A real smash hit'

Isabelle reflected on his words as she tidied the flat and checked to see that Bienvenue was sleeping peacefully.

Then, opening her portable typewriter, she began to write.

Chapter 3:

LUNCH WITH A LION

Morbignan La Crèbe, Thursday evening

The *Salle des Fêtes* had never been so crammed. Every seat was taken, and Joséphine had to beg extra chairs from *l'Estaminet,* crowding them into the aisles despite the Health and Safety grumblings of Papa Pardieu. Morbignan's most celebrated daughter had returned in triumph from her mysterious exile of some twenty years, and the villagers were going to get to meet a real live literary lion.

Ysabel de la Fontaine's talk was a success. Gasps and giggles punctuated her words as the listeners recognised their friends and neighbours (though never themselves), deftly caricatured in her readings from *Les Aventures de Glou-glou, Les Malheurs de Glou-glou* and – her newest book – *Glou-glou, ce Héros.*

Only the central figure was missing from the *Salle des Fêtes*: *Glou-glou* himself. Gaspard Petit had no interest in hearing the ramblings of some random female, however comical her books were said to be. No matter: there were plenty among the audience that day who were looking forward to enlightening him. No-one suspected the final bombshell that Ysabel was preparing to detonate.

Morbignan And St Rémy Les Cevennes, Friday

The day following the talk dawned hot, blue and gold. But then the rain had come, as the southern summer rain will come, out of nowhere. When Ysabel set out to keep her lunch date with Gaspard, the sun was shining and the sky was that deep purple blue that only a Languedoc summer knows. But as the taxi climbed out of Morbignan she could see the black clouds gathering above the sprawl of St Rémy in the distance, and she knew they were in for a storm.

Sure enough, by the time they drew up outside *Le Lion d'Or* the rain was torrential – hurtling to the ground and bouncing back off the steaming pavement. Cursing her lack of umbrella, Ysabel gripped the flowery concoction that was her hat, and dashed for the restaurant.

Chang, the proprietor, was all smiles and bows. What an honour, said his twinkling black eyes, what a privilege to have the famous author at his table. He could see the kitchen door was ajar: his wife Soo-ki was agog to see their distinguished guest, though little Nyam Nyam couldn't conceal her disappointment: she had been promised a lion but all she saw was a tall woman with a flowery hat perched on a complicated confection of red-brown curls.

Chang proudly led Ysabel to the best table in the room, already set for three, with delicate enamelled bowls, red-lacquered chopsticks and a vase containing two lotus flowers and a spray of fern. Ysabel allowed herself to be seated and submitted to the flourish with which the head waiter shook out her damask napkin and laid it across her lap.

'Perhaps Madame would like a drink while she awaits her guests?' Chang murmured.

'Thank you, Chang, no. Just some tea, if you please.'

She glanced at the tiny gold watch on her wrist and tutted. Gaspard was late. Well, she shouldn't be surprised: neither manners nor punctuality were his strong suit.

What's she up to?

On his way to St Rémy, Gaspard was in a fizz of anticipation and doubt. Why had this woman invited him to lunch? No-one formally invited anyone to lunch in Morbignan. You just dropped in to someone's kitchen around *midi* and looked hopeful, or else the invitation was issued casually over a drink at *L'Estaminet*. And why had Ysabel suggested *Le Lion d'Or*, the swankiest Chinese restaurant in St Rémy? What was she after? She said it was to thank him for picking her up at the station, and volunteering to take her back to Montpellier at the end of her stay. It seemed excessive to Gaspard.

Then there was that business of the laughter. Although Gaspard knew who Ysabel was – he could hardly have avoided knowing it, these past few days – he had only a dim notion of what she wrote. Suddenly, ever

136

since Ysabel's arrival in their midst, his neighbours had taken to pointing and giggling when they encountered him in the *boulangerie* or the bar. Was this woman mocking in some way? And if so, how? Today, he resolved, he would get to the bottom of it.

Chang had brought Ysabel's tea, and a plate of miniature spring rolls as an *amuse bouche* while she waited for her guest. She bit into one and almost cried out: her teeth had met something hard and gritty. She held her napkin to her lips and discreetly ejected a small stone – clearly the bean sprouts hadn't been washed carefully enough. Chang would be mortified, she thought, glancing round the restaurant, but thankfully there was no sign of him.

Her eye was caught by a small screen placed high on the wall: the CCTV camera, monitoring the restaurant entrance, showed her the ungainly form of Gaspard lurching in out of the rain. He had hardly made an effort for the occasion. His tee shirt was more grey than white and his belly slithered over the waistband of his baggy jeans. Pinned to his chest was that enamel pin with the image of a black cat on it.

Ysabel sighed. He had been so handsome in his youth. Unpolished, yes, but delicious. Her mind drifted back to the teenage village girl swept away by the rough good looks and Harley Davidson of the village ne'er do well.

She smiled as he approached her table.

'Monsieur Petit, I am so glad you could join us.' She extended her hand, which he ignored.

'Us?' he wondered. There was nobody at the table apart from this rather strange woman. He dropped into a chair, surveying the elegant table setting with disgust.

'Here! Ching-chang, or whatever your name is,' he shouted, snapping his fingers.

Chang hurried up; he didn't miss Ysabel's look of embarrassment and apology, but his own face was professionally impassive.

'Monsieur? Is there something I can help you with?'

'Take away this stuff and bring me something proper to eat with. I like my food served on a plate, with a knife and fork, none of this foreign rubbish.'

'Certainly, Monsieur, at once,' said Chang smoothly.

'Perhaps I have made a mistake?' Ysabel enquired. 'Perhaps you would have preferred a Macdonald's, or we could have gone to a *Buffalo Grill*?'

Irony was lost on Gaspard.

'No, this is fine. I like Chinese food, but I can't be doing with all this flim-flam. Why can't they eat like normal people?'

Ysabel ordered; while the food was being brought Gaspard kept glancing curiously at the third table setting.

'Who...' he began, just as Ysabel was saying

'I have a reason for inviting you today...'

She stopped, noticing his attention had drifted to the large gilt framed mirror on the crimson flock wall behind her. His piggy eyes lit up.

Ysabel rose to welcome a slim, auburn haired young woman making her way towards their table.

'This is...' she began, but Gaspard was on his feet, enclosing the young woman's hand in a massive paw and leering into her face.

'Monsieur Petit,' said Ysabel formally, 'may I present...' She leaned forward and her lips almost brushed his ear as she murmured an introduction.

Gaspard's jaw dropped as he stood looking from the older woman to the younger.

Chapter 4:

FISTICUFFS AT A PARTY

Morbignan La Crèbe, Saturday

For a man who had said he didn't want a party, Thierry was the life and soul. Presiding over a vast punch bowl he welcomed one, welcomed all.

'*Salut, Romain!*' he cried as yet another calloused hand thumped on his shoulder with a hearty '*Félicitations, mon ami!*'

On this glorious Saturday evening, just five days short of *Le Quatorze* – the annual Bastille Day celebrations – the village basked in splendour. By half past seven the sun was beginning to sink into a green sky behind the crumbling church tower. The chattering swifts had gone to roost and the first bats fluttered out into the dusk; in Céleste and Thierry's little house above the river the festivities roared on.

Richard Patterson stood by the window, glancing down to where the party had spilled out on to the path, and beyond to the uneven and weed-choked stone steps which snaked down behind the church to the riverbank. Martha, Patterson's wife, was, as usual, at the centre of a lively crowd. And, as usual, Visitor sat at her feet, the little dog gazing up adoringly at the *vol au vent* in her mistress's hand. Beside Patterson stood his closest friend, Bernard Durand. They made an incongruous pair: the tall, thin, balding English poet and the stocky, broad-shouldered French former detective.

The music changed and the voice of Georges Brassens belted out his famous song, *Les Copains d'Abord*. Seizing the moment, P'tit Gui and Matthieu the plumber grabbed Thierry by each arm and processed round the room in a mad approximation of a can-can. Everyone cheered wildly when François Peitavy, the village's pompous former *notaire,* capered behind them, twirling the ends of his moustache. It was amazing what a few glasses of *rosé* could do.

But every silver lining has its cloud. Lurking in a corner – because it would have been rude not to invite him – was Gaspard Petit, the most hated man in the village. If he had set out deliberately to antagonise every one of his neighbours, Petit could not have been more successful. Nursing his glass – his fourth, to Céleste's certain knowledge - he stared round the room from beneath belligerent brows.

Euphoric on a cloud of music and wine, the dancers didn't notice their unpleasant neighbour. Until, that is, Peitavy, eyes closed and lost in the moment, tripped over Gaspard's size 11 boots and almost landed in his lap. Gaspard leapt up with a roar, tumbling Peitavy to the floor.

'You clumsy oaf,' he yelled, jus as Peitavy protested,

'Why can't you keep your big feet to yourself?'

The two men glared at each other.

'I know all about you, you bastard,' Peitavy snarled. 'You betrayed my daughter and then abandoned your wife and snuck off to Pars like the cowardly villain you are. One of these days someone is going to make you pay, and that someone might just be me.'

'I'll see you in hell first, you bungling bureaucrat!' Gaspard lunged at Peitavy, fists clenched just as Peitavy threw a wild punch at his head. Ducking easily under the ex-*notaire's* flailing arm, Gaspard stepped in and grabbed him by the shoulders. For a moment it looked as if the scene might get ugly, then:

'Now, now, now!' Bernard Durand's voice boomed across the room. 'Peitavy! Petit! This is a celebration, not a brawl. How dare you disrespect Thierry at his birthday party, and Céleste and her daughters who have created this wonderful *fête* for us all to enjoy?'

'Oh, it's the great detective,' Petit sneered. 'Well, you weren't so high and mighty in Paris all those years ago, sprawled out in your *culottes* for all to see.'

Durand went beet-red.

'Why you…' he charged at Gaspard, who stepped back, laughing at the memory of past triumphs.

Chapter 5:

LILI'S JEWELS

Paris, 1998

The policeman berated

'Aaaargh!'

Bernard Durand opened one eye and hastily closed it again. The sunlight was no respecter of persons: it cheerfully bullied its way through the meagre curtains of his bedroom, forcing him to fling one arm across his face in protest. Despite his very best efforts, bits and pieces of yesterday's humiliation rose to the surface of his consciousness.

Commandant Leboeuf had not been pleased, and he'd let it be known. Summoning Durand to his office, he'd glared at him across the expanse of his polished rosewood desk.

'Well, Durand, what have you got to report?' he'd barked. 'There was another incident last night. This time it was the wife of the Mayor. The Mayor, Durand. As you can imagine he is asking some very pointed questions. And what have you done to catch this impertinent thief? Nothing.'

'But, *Monsieur le Commandant*,' Durand began, but the senior officer overrode him.

'But? There are no buts, Durand. You are a useless specimen of an officer of the law. Seven times this *salaud* (bastard) has struck, and not at insignificant people, oh no. The Vietnamese ambassador is furious, and *Député* Marceau is demanding I be sacked. You can be sure that your job is a lot less safe than mine. Now get out there and catch this thief or you'll be on traffic duties until hell freezes over.'

141

Smarting from this severe tongue-lashing, Durand had done the only thing possible: he had gone out and got right royally drunk.

Lili

As the young policeman was waking to the mother of all hangovers, across the city another awakening was about to bring wails of dismay.

Lili *la Voix* was the toast of Paris. Born Liliane Dumont in a genteel suburb of Paris, Lili was known for two things: her sunny nature, and her love of singing. She was the first to put her hand up in school when there was talk of a recital. At the morning assembly she sang *La Marseillaise*, the national anthem, with fervour and great energy. She adored her music lessons and practised each vocal exercise assiduously, bringing tears to the eyes of her fond parents. Alas, they were not tears of joy.

Truth to tell, Liliane had a perfectly terrible voice. Her teachers, knowing her enthusiasm, tried to be kind. M. Dattas, the choirmaster, didn't have the heart to exclude her. Instead, he urged her merely to mime the words the other children were singing.

'Your voice is too rich, *ma petite*, he would cajole her. 'You put the others in the shade.'

Then, the age of 13, Liliane found her voice. Or, more precisely, she lost it. Laid low by a terrible flu that swept through the school, Liliane was silent for a week. When her speech returned it was only a croak; undaunted, she returned to school the next day, belting out '*Allons enfants de la patrie...*' at assembly with her usual gusto. One by one the others fell silent, stunned by the *basso profundo* issuing from Liliane's mouth.

As one teacher later described it in the staff room: 'It sounded like a cross between Edith Piaf and a coal scuttle being dragged across a concrete floor.'

Did they but know it, Liliane had set her foot on the path that was to lead to international stardom.

When she was 16, the Lycée decided to stage a new musical version of *La Belle au Bois Dormant* (*Sleeping Beauty*). Taking the libretto from the original Perrault fairy tale, M Dattas, now the head teacher, composed an original score with a dozen songs, to accommodate as many eager young vocalists as possible.

142

Liliane, of course, yearned to play the title role. Her petite frame, long blond hair and blue eyes certainly qualified her for the part; her voice did not. M. Dattas consoled her.

'Never mind, *mon chou*, I have a very special role in mind for you.' He handed Liliane a marked score. 'What do you say to Carabosse?'

Traditionally, the wicked fairy has very little to say beyond pronouncing her curse on the sleeping baby princess. M. Dattas had changed all that.

On opening night, an audience of some 300 parents, brothers, sisters, teachers and assorted well-wishers gathered expectantly in the school auditorium. The play proceeded along conventional lines until, just as the last good fairy was about to bestow her gift, the stage suddenly went dark to the crash of thunder and a screech as of demons. When the lights came up the audience gasped, then simultaneously burst into laughter.

Instead of the expected crone, with wild hair and a warty nose, there in the spotlight stood a pretty little girl. Her blonde hair cascaded from beneath a jewel-encrusted diadem. Her wide blue eyes surveyed the gathering. Then, with her hands clasped demurely before her, she took a deep breath and launched into the song M. Dattas had written specially for her: '*Je te souhaite*'.

Gleefully, in that inimitable voice, Carabosse described all the terrible things she wished on the baby, culminating in the prediction that on her 21st birthday she would prick her finger on a needle and die.

On a final shriek of '*tout ça je te shouhaite*' ('all this I wish you') she lunged towards the cradle, scattering the terrified courtiers. There was an eye-watering flash of light, followed by darkness, and the curtain came down.

For a moment there was total silence, then a roar of applause, catcalls and whistles swept through the auditorium. Seizing the moment and Liliane's hand, M. Dattas dashed on to the stage; standing before the curtain they took their bows.

After the play, the classroom designated as the girls' dressing room was abuzz with congratulations. Marcel and Suzanne Dumont hugged their daughter fiercely and even Jimi, her 12-year-old brother, managed to mutter '*pas mal, Lili*' before rushing off to join his special crony Simon, who had played the first footman.

Among the mélée no-one particularly noticed a small, tubby man in a camel hair coat who drew Liliane's parents to one side. After a few

143

muttered words he left, but not before pressing a business card into Marcel's moist palm.

'Who was that man you were talking to, *Papa*?' Liliane wanted to know.

'His name is Maurice Perrin. He's some kind of cousin of your head teacher's. He came along tonight because M. Dattas said he would see something extraordinary. You.' Her father extracted the card from his waistcoat pocket.

'Perrin runs *Le Coq Affamé* – it's a club in the *huitième arrondissement*. It's not very well known but it is becoming popular. He wanted to know if I would allow you to sing there. I said no, of course.'

'*Papa*,' Liliane began on a wail, but her father held up his hand.

'Liliane, *j'ai dit non*. I said no. You are much too young to be in a place like that. You will stay at school and finish your studies. Do well in your *Bac* and we shall see.'

Liliane sulked for a week, but *Papa's* word was law. Gradually the excitement of the school play was forgotten in the intensive round of studies Liliane needed to prepare for her *Baccalauréat*. When she eventually emerged from the examinations, armed with exceptional grades, she departed for the university of Montpellier to study marine biology. And, like thousands of students before her, she was also enthusiastically exploring another kind of biology, though she was careful not to tell her parents about that.

Never short of suitors, Liliane happily played the field for a year before allowing herself to be won by her classmate Marco – half-Italian, half-French and wholly her devoted slave.

Marco was a musician – a bass guitarist in a student folk-rock band called *Les Copins du Port*. This was a nod towards the Languedoc's famous son, the singer Georges Brassens, whose best-loved song was *Les Copins d'Abord* (mates first). The band's name also reflected the fact that most of their gigs were in tiny harbourside cafés where, like as not, their "fee" consisted of a bowl of whatever the establishment was serving that day and as much *vin du pays* as they could drink.

Les Copins was fronted by Amélie, a philosophy student with drop-dead good looks and a voice nobody would write home about. But, and this was important, Amélie was the *petite amie* of Gérard, the band's founder, lead guitarist and manager.

144

Everything changed the day Amélie and Gérard had a spectacular row. Gérard had, it is true, been paying rather a lot of attention to Marco's blonde girlfriend. Amélie had, it is true, been flirting with a suave café owner who promised her stardom in exchange for just a little kindness.

Whatever the reason, the resentments boiled up to the point where irrevocable insults were exchanged and Amélie departed in a swirl of black hair and *Anaïs Anaïs*. This would have been unfortunate at any time: on this particular morning it was catastrophic. Gérard had secured for the band an important appearance at the *toro piscine* in Palavas-les-Flots. This was a much-loved tourist attraction involving bull calves and a large inflatable paddling pool, invariably accompanied by live music from a local band. Gérard had done a lot of schmoozing and bought not a few *demis* and *petits pastis* to get them this prestigious gig. And now here he was without a vocalist. Casting about for a solution, he had an idea.

'Marco,' he began, 'your girlfriend is a singer, isn't she?'

Marco looked at him dubiously. 'Have you heard Liliane sing? He voice is... unusual, to say the least.'

Gérard was not to be deterred.

'I'd say her voice is different. What's wrong with that? Do you know the American singer Tom Waits? She sounds a lot like him, and he isn't doing too badly.'

Liliane was beside herself. A real performance in a real band! True, the band would be competing with excited tourists playing at matadors, the cries of vendors vaunting churros and *barbe à papa* – candy floss – and the wails of a distant fairground organ. It mattered not: this was her first professional gig and she was going to make the most of it.

'We'll have to find a new name for you,' mused Gérard. 'Liliane Dumont isn't the coolest of names for a folk singer.'

'My family always called me Lili,' Liliane said.

'Yes, that might do,' said Gérard. 'We'll call you Lili...Lili...' he paused, scratching at his sparse goatee. Inspiration struck. 'It's your voice that makes you who you are. We'll call you *Lili la Voix*.'

And in that moment a star was born.

Lili the Voice made her début with another classic Georges Brassens song, *Chanson pour l'Auvergnat*, making it her own from that day forward. And, from that day forward, every time she sang it, she heard the funfair noises, smelled the warm sugar of frying doughnuts, felt the scorch of the July evening sun on her shoulders as her imagination took her back to that first time in the little seaside town of Palavas-les-Flots.

Now, waking in her luxurious hotel near the Madeleine, she was blissfully aware that Paris was at her feet. Stretching like a cat, she relived last night's triumph at the *Paris Olympe* and the breathless journey that had taken her here. That first performance in Palavas had swiftly brought her more engagements, and a professional manager. Marine biology was forgotten. Marco, with lingering regret, was forgotten. Lili's return to Paris had catapulted her into a social whirl of artists and musicians, and a life of wealth and luxury that Liliane Dumont could only have dreamed of.

Languorously she turned her head on the pillow - and screamed. Her scarlet leather jewel case stood empty on the reproduction Louis XV bureau. Her priceless emeralds were gone.

'*Madame? Vous êtes malade?*' The maid had heard her screams and came rushing in after a perfunctory knock.

Lili was in hysterics. '*La police. Appelez la police*,' she moaned.

The policeman smitten

The telephone buzzed through Bernard Durand's head like a pneumatic drill. Groaning, he peered at his watch: 7:30 am. As he picked up the receiver his boss was already in full spate. 'Durand? Durand, what are you doing? Get your lazy carcase over to the Hotel Intercontinental *tout de suite*. There has been another incident.'

Thirty minutes later Durand was walking into the scented and softly lit hotel suite of *Lili la Voix*. Although, at the great age of 28, he considered himself a hardened professional, he couldn't help feeling just a little star-struck. The room was immaculate. A pair of fur-trimmed slippers stood neatly side by side, like prim schoolgirls, beneath the bed. An *eau-de-nil* silk robe patterned with green and blue dragons hung from a hook on the bathroom door. An array of lotions and potions stood regimented on the glass-topped dressing table on which not a trace of dust or a speck of powder could be seen.

146

The only things out of place were a scarlet jewel case sprawled open across the bureau, and a rumpled coverlet on the bed beneath which a tangle of blonde hair sobbed piteously.

'Madame?' he began tentatively. Then, more loudly, 'Madame Lili?'

'Mzzl' came from the heap of bedclothes.

'*Pardon*, Madame?'

'Mademoiselle,' said Lili more clearly.

The girl sat up, raking scarlet-tipped fingers through her curls. Durand gazed into a pair of cornflower blue eyes and was lost.

Chapter 6

GASPARD AND THE POLICEMAN

Paris 1998

'Bonjour, Mademoiselle,' he said hoarsely: his throat had gone unaccountably dry. 'Can you tell me exactly, please, what time you got back to your hotel room, and what you did then?'

'I must have got up to my room about two,' Lili said. We went for supper at Maxim's after the show, then Pierre, my manager, and his wife came back to the hotel for a nightcap.'

'And did you put your jewel case away or leave it out?'

'I put it away.' Lili was emphatic. 'I always insist that my hotel room has a safe. Some of my jewels are valuable, especially the emeralds. They were a gift from my grandmother and I wouldn't lose them for anything. I always make absolutely sure they are locked away, no matter how late it is. The safe is over there, behind the bathroom door.'

Durand strolled across the room. The safe door was closed but not locked. Taking a handkerchief from his pocket, he wound it round his fingers before easing the door open. The safe was empty apart from a postcard, showing a black cat sitting on a wall. Turning the card over, Durand read the words he expected to find there:

'*Le Petit Chat vous remercie.*'

'The little cat says thank you'. Durand felt his heart sink. The Little Cat, as the thief called himself, had struck again.

The ironic message, the image of the cat, the surname – all added up to one villain: Gaspard Petit. Gaspard Petit had been a thorn in Bernard Durand's side since they had both entered the *école maternelle* at the age of five. They had been born within days of each other in the little Languedoc village of Morbignan la Crèbe. But while Gaspard had emerged from his mother, red-faced and bawling, at an impressive 4.2 kilos, Durand was a slender, pale and quiet baby half his weight.

It soon became clear, however that what Bernard lacked in bulk he made up for in brains. As a schoolboy he was always one of the first to put up his hand in class, and his lively wit was earning him the respect of his teachers and fellow pupils. Sadly, though, neither intelligence nor wit protected him from the bullying taunts and heavy fists of Gaspard Petit.

Paris awaits

At the age of 18 Durand took his guitar and a baguette stuffed with jambon and *Pélardon*, the local goat's cheese, and set off for Paris to make his fame and fortune. The dream barely outlasted the sandwich. No impresario, no record company magnate swooped in to carry him off to stardom from the left-bank cellar café where, for a plate of couscous and a handful of euros, he nightly massacred the songs of Brassens and Brel.

It was Bernard's great good fortune that the restaurant was staffed with illegal immigrants and didn't possess a music licence. The day that the police raided was a turning point for him. Seduced by their stern voices, their quasi-military uniforms, the sexy bulge of their holstered pistols, he decided there and then to join the *Sûreté*.

And so far he hadn't made a bad fist of it. His arrest record was impressive and the operation he had led to catch a gang of bank robbers had earned him a minor commendation. At 28, he was on track for high office — until Le Petit Chat came into the picture.

This daring thief targeted the wealthiest citizens, the most high-profile of victims. Slipping in and out of their homes like a ghost, he selected only the finest jewels, melting away long before the police arrived on the scene — but not before he had left his ironic calling-card. At the scene of each crime a picture postcard would be found. On its front, the picture of a black cat sitting on a wall; on the back, the words *'Le Petit Chat vous remercie'*.

Despite the attempts of the police to keep the story under wraps, it wasn't long before *Le Parisien* got hold of it; soon the exploits of Le Petit Chat were the talk of Paris. Who was this mysterious cat burglar, a modern-day version of Raffles, the legendary jewel thief?

Bernard Durand, on the other hand, thought he knew perfectly well who Le Petit Chat was. He remembered the day the hulking Gaspard Petit had arrived back from the summer vacation to begin the new school year in *troisième*, proudly sporting a nascent moustache. Alas, the effect was not what he had hoped.

'*Hé, Gaspard, tu as un chat sous le nez?*' shouted Marc Sériex, the school comedian. Twenty-two fourteen-year-old boys shrieked with laughter, falling to the ground with exaggerated mirth. It wasn't so much the vision of the unfortunate Gaspard having a cat on his upper lip that had them wetting their trousers, but the lewder meaning of the word chat – or, as one might say in English, pussy.

Furious and humiliated, Gaspard fled from the playground and was absent from school for the rest of the week. The following Monday, though, there came a transformation. Gaspard swaggered into the playground resplendent in a battered black leather jacket, clearly the product of the *frip'* – the second-hand stall in the local market. On the lapel was an enamel pin badge with the image of a black cat. Gaspard Petit had owned Le Chat.

Now, fourteen years later in Paris, Durand reflected, a 'cat' burglar calling himself Petit could only be that inky schoolboy, re-inventing himself in the capital. And yet he had niggling doubts. The Gaspard Petit he had known in Morbignan was not notable either for his brains or his finesse. Could he really have morphed into the suave, dangerous, glamorous thief who had been holding all Paris to ransom? Certainly not without guidance, Durand concluded.

Even before Le Petit Chat had made such a name for himself, there had been a spate of audacious jewellery thefts in the city. And there had been hints: the words les *sacrés jumeaux* (those blasted twins) were beginning to be whispered in the press and in the corridors of the *Sûreté*. If these elusive burglars had taken Gaspard under their wing – or, more likely, were using him for their own advantage – that would go a long way to explaining Le Petit Chat.

None of this was any help, though. Knowing who Le Petit Chat was and actually catching him were two different things. And Bernard couldn't help thinking that his old schoolmate was taunting him. He was to be proved right.

As he left Lili La Voix's hotel suite, a plan was forming in his mind.

A piece of string

Back at the police station, Durand stared at the large-scale Paris street map on his office wall. It was studded with seven red-topped drawing

150

pins. Thoughtfully, the young policeman took a box of drawing pins from his desk and shook out one more, affixing it to the map at the site of the Hotel Intercontinental.   Then, employing the most high-tech of methods, he began to connect the pins with string. When he was done, he gave a 'voila!' of satisfaction: the strings all intersected at one point, in the *sixième arrondissement*. This must surely be the hub of Le Petit Chat's operations, he mused.

It took him two days walking the streets of the *sixième* to find what he was looking for: a modest – not to say seedy – hotel tucked up a narrow side street. The concierge, persuaded by the suggestion of a couple of ten-euro notes, readily identified Gaspard Petit from an old school photo Bernard had dug out from a box on the top of his wardrobe.

'He's older than that,' the concierge said, considering the 14-year-old features, 'but that's him all right. Shall I tell him you are asking for him?'

Hastily turning down the man's offer, Durand left. He had plans to make.

Rightly assuming that Gaspard Petit would be out about his unlawful business during the hours of darkness, he returned to the hotel at 9pm. A quick flash of his *Police Nationale* badge persuaded the night porter, a grimy individual with a dewdrop on the end of his nose and the evidence of many a meal on his shirt, to show him Petit's room and let him in with the pass key.

Although the furniture had seen better days and the curtains were ragged, the room was clean and tidy. A side table held a wilting cactus in a pot within a chipped green outer pot, and a battered cabin trunk stood against the wall. Durand lifted the trunk's lid and gave a cry of triumph. Lying atop a treasure trove of jewels and *objets d'art* were Lili's emeralds.

A footfall alerted him: someone was coming up the stairs. There was no escape, nowhere to hide. Grabbing the emeralds, he lifted the cactus and thrust the necklace into its outer pot, replacing the plant and turning back into the room just as the door opened.

For a breathless second the adversaries confronted each other, then Petit roared, rushed at the policeman, and knocked him to the floor. His head hit the corner of the trunk and he knew no more.

An insistent light was trying to pry his eyelids apart, boring its way into his brain. Durand groaned and rolled over in the bed. It was hard, and very cold: it almost felt like stone. Dimly he became aware of voices, of laughter; as he dragged his eyes open he could see booted feet surrounding him.

'*Qu'squispasse?*' he groaned, 'whass going on?' at which point the laughter became louder. Disobeying his body, which was screaming at him to curl into a ball and nurse his aching head in his arms, Durand sat up. He was not at home in his familiar bed, but the surroundings were equally familiar: he was on the steps of the police station. And no wonder he was cold: he was clad only in his boxers. His Star Wars boxers. As a colleague, kinder than the rest, helped him to his feet, something fell out of the waistband. It was a small card with an image of a cat on it. On the back, when Durand could focus, were written the words: '*Le Petit Chat vous demande pardon.*' The Little Cat begs your pardon.

The insolence of the apology was breath-taking. Crimson with fury, Bernard Durand swore vengeance.

Crimson with fury, Commandant Leboeuf berated the hapless policeman, now respectably clad in borrowed uniform trousers and a spare shirt.

'You let him get away?' bellowed the *commandant*. 'You actually found the criminal and you let him get away? I'll have you on school patrol for the rest of your career, you useless specimen of a policeman.'

'*Oui, mon commandant.*' Durand could only hang his head: the reprimand was well deserved, he supposed. Truth to tell, the events of the previous evening were hazy. He remembered his triumph at finding Petit's lair at last. He remembered the burglar rushing at him, and then nothing more. But –- wait! One small, insistent memory was nagging at him. Something to do with jewels. Lili's jewels.

Durand ran the gauntlet of his colleagues' sympathetic stares back to his desk, where he slumped, his head in his hands. A kindly desk sergeant placed a strong black coffee at his elbow; Durand thanked him with a vague wave of the hand. Headache and humiliation forgotten, he was thinking furiously.

Six hours later, he was once again walking up the steps to the hotel in the *sixième*. The night porter's eyes widened: surely the *flic* would be very, very angry. Surely he had come to arrest the man who had helped bundle him into a cabin trunk? As he began to babble his excuses and denials, Durand held up an imperious hand.

'The key,' he demanded. 'Give me the key to that room.'

'But monsieur – *officier* – that gentleman is no longer there. He, er, departed last night…'

'Never mind. Give me the key at once.'

Clutching the key, Bernard Durand made his way up to the room that had been Gaspard Petit's. It was as he remembered it: the mismatched furniture, the ragged curtains, only the cabin trunk was missing. Durand couldn't have cared less: there, on the listing side table, stood the plant in its green *cache-pot*. Carefully, he lifted the plant from its holder. A brighter green sparkled beneath: Lili's emeralds.

Policeman in paradise

At four o'clock Durand was in the sumptuous lobby of the Hotel Intercontinental.

'Madame Lili?' he enquired of the haughty concierge.

'Madame is resting. She has a performance this evening and has particularly asked not to be disturbed,' was the disdainful reply.

The policeman handed the concierge his card.

'Please send this up to Madame Lili and tell her I have something to impart which will be of great interest to her. I think she will receive me.'

Reluctantly, the concierge summoned a bellboy and entrusted him with the message, and within minutes Durand was once again in the scented boudoir of the famous singer. With a certain theatricality he withdrew from his pocket a package wrapped in tissue paper.

'Can it be? Have you really found my emeralds?' Lili flung her arms around his neck, covering his face with kisses. He did not resist.

After the first raptures were over, Lili poured them both a glass of champagne from a bottle standing ready in an ice bucket on a side table.

'Now,' she demanded, 'tell me how you did it.'

Bernard Durand spun the story out as long as he could, enchanted by the blue eyes which never left his face. The part about the boxer shorts he omitted. When the tale was concluded, they went on to discuss other things, many other things.

When it was time for Lili to change for her performance, Durand left her. As he walked down the carpeted steps to the hotel lobby he was whistling a Georges Brassens song: *J'ai rendez-vous avec vous*. I have a date with you.

Chapter 7:

'AT LEAST I WENT TO PARIS'

Morbignan La Crèbe, Saturday

Patterson and Peitavy were hanging on every word as Durand finished his tale. To his credit, the Englishman had resisted the temptation to howl with glee at the image of his dignified friend sprawled out in his underdrawers on the police station steps.

'Go on, laugh,' said the policeman good-naturedly. 'I know it's funny, and I can laugh about it too, now. You know, it was years till I told Lili the full story, but when I did she just smiled and said, "Well, you had the last laugh, didn't you?" She was right: if it hadn't been for that fellow we would never have met.'

'Yes, it turned out OK for you,' Peitavy commented, 'but things didn't go so well for my daughter. At least, at first…'

He closed one eye in a suggestive wink.

'No, I'm saying no more. You will see what you will see.'

Gaspard had been watching the three men, suspecting that they were talking about him. A burst of laughter galvanised him out of his chair, and he swaggered over to them.

'Who invited you to join a private conversation?' Peitavy snarled. 'We've been hearing all about your goings-on in Paris, and now you're back here where you began, and what have you got to show for it? There's a nasty shock in store for you, mark my words.'

'At least I went to Paris,' Gaspard retorted, 'unlike you, stuck in your muddy little village for all of your life. And I had a successful career there, too, which is more than you can say for yourself.'

Durand raised a sceptical eyebrow. 'A successful career? Do you know, that doesn't sound like you, Gaspard. Oh, yes, I know all about *Le Petit Chat*…' Gaspard smirked.

'But,' the policeman continued, 'somehow I doubt the success you boast of was all your own. Perhaps you had a little help?'

He wasn't wrong.

Chapter 8:

GASPARD AND THE COUSINS

Paris, December 1997

They made him feel like a country cousin, these sophisticated thirty-somethings in their Armani suits and gold jewellery.

And, indeed, that was just what he was. Only two days earlier, Gaspard Petit had arrived in the capital, bewildered by the noise and the crush of people who thronged the boulevards. He'd found refuge in a small hotel in the *sixième arrondissement*, neither elegant not particularly clean, but it was all his budget could afford. After depositing his duffel bag on the bed, he went back down to the lobby to find the hotel's one telephone. Smoothing a much-folded letter, he made his call.

'Yes,' said his cousin on the other end of the line, 'we will meet you at ten o'clock tomorrow at *Le Café des Arts.*'

The next morning, Jean-Luc and Jean-Marc regarded Gaspard out of identical dark eyes as he sipped his *demi* and tried to look at home in this fashionable café near the Arc de Triomphe.

'So,' said Jean-Marc, lighting his third Gitane, 'you have finally made the break from your dreary little village and come to join your cousins in the bright lights. Or did your dreary little wife get tired of you and kick you out?'

Gaspard scowled.

'Not so much the wife, though she's dreary enough,' he answered. 'But the Papa – awful man! No sense of family. I did him the great honour of marrying his daughter. I was quite a catch, you know,' he boasted, unaware of the smile that passed between the twins.

'And Papa's not short of a franc or two, so naturally you'd expect him to bring me into his nice little wine business on the management side. Bur oh, no, he expected me to work in the damn vines like a lowly peasant. All the money was tied up tight for Mimi and any brats she might produce.

'And as for Mimi, well you'd expect a woman to speak up for her husband, wouldn't you? But no, she sided with Papa. "It's for our children," she said. Well, she can whistle for children, I wasn't going to hang about in that dreary village, as you so aptly call it, to be treated like a serf.'

Jean Luc and Jean Marc exchanged a look. 'Well, there's plenty of *fric* (dosh) to be had in Paris if you're prepared to learn the business,' they promised.

'Lead me to it!' Gaspard's eyes gleamed with greed.

'Not so fast, little cousin,' said Jean-Marc. 'You have quite a bit to learn. 'First and foremost, we have to get you out of those provincial clothes.'

Gaspard blinked. He had thought he cut quite a dash in his distressed leather jacket and fashionably battered jeans.

'Here.' Jean-Luc tossed a bundle of 500-franc notes on to the café table. 'Get yourself a decent suit. You look like a burglar in that outfit.' The twins burst out laughing; Gaspard couldn't see the joke but feared it was at his expense.

'Tomorrow is *Réveillon*, New Year's Eve,' said Jean-Luc. '*Le tout Paris* will be out on the streets, partying at Sacré Coeur or watching the fireworks off the Pont Neuf. That's when we go to work. You'll need a dinner jacket too: we're going into high society.'

'Do you think he'll do?' queried Jean Luc after Gaspard had left the table in search of the stylish yet affordable tailor they had recommended.

'Bah, who knows?' his brother shrugged. 'But we have two scenarios here. Either he makes a complete mess of things, in which he'll get arrested and we'll disappear with no-one the wiser.'

'Or,' Jean-Luc cut in, 'he'll turn out to be brilliant and...'

'...we'll be all the richer' the twins finished as one, laughing.

'He has one great advantage,' Jean-Marc went on. 'He is not, yet, "known to the police" – especially that interfering idiot Durand. That one is getting a bit too close for comfort. And, come to think of it, Petit is a good bit younger than we are, not to mention' — he patted his *embonpoint* affectionately — 'a good bit slimmer. He'll worm his way into much smaller spaces than we could these days.'

It was true, the wages of sin had been kind to the brothers, sitting sleekly about their hips and on their well-groomed jowls.

Gaspard was almost unrecognisable when the three met again at noon the next day. He slouched to the café table in a dove grey three-piece suit, a matching cap pulled rakishly over one eye. Gone were the grubby white Nike Air-Max trainers, replaced by classic Ted-Baker-style black brogues. An excess of Aramis hung about him like a miasma. Only the wide tie splashed with tropical flowers in startling blues, yellows and greens betrayed his own secret preferences.

The cousins took it all in. Wincing slightly, Jean-Marc fished from his pocket a slim navy blue tie with a subtle stripe.

'Put this on and lose the stupid hat. Then you'll just about pass muster' was his only comment.

Diamonds, dancing, disaster

Sylvie de Lacoste was all of a flutter. Tonight was New Year's Eve and she was about to go to her first grown-up dance at a grand hotel.

'Will this do, *ma tante?*' she asked anxiously, holding up her best dress, a rather creased dusky rose affair with last year's sleeves. Madame La Marquise de Saint-Esprit sighed but resisted an eye roll.

'*Non, non, ma petite,*' she scolded her niece. 'We can do better than that. Madame Félix will be attending us presently with a selection of suitable gowns. The George V is the finest hotel in the finest city in all of Europe if not the world. The *Réveillon* will be a glittering affair attended by all the great and the good. Remember that and mind your manners tonight.'

Like Gaspard, Sylvie was new in Paris: she, too, had arrived only yesterday, from the small southern town of Clermont l'Hérault, some 25 km from Gaspard's own village. Unaware that their lives were soon to brush, if only tangentially, she could barely contain her excitement about the coming ball.

By eight o'clock the two ladies, following the ministrations of Madame Félix, were ready to be gowned in splendour. As befitted her youth, Sylvie had been allowed to choose a pale eau-de-nil frock which flattered her slim figure and displayed a modest, though becoming, décolletage. The Marquise had lent her a delicate white-gold chain from which depended one flawless teardrop sapphire. Tiny sapphires nestled in her ears, behind which her aunt had dabbed a whisper of *Arpège.* She was ready.

Not so her aunt. Fret though Sylvie might, Madame la Marquise would proceed at her own pace. Rising at last from her dressing table, where she had paid lengthy attention to her face and neck, she allowed her maid to help her into the voluminous folds of grenadine velvet that Madame Félix had pinned and tucked and fussed over not four hours earlier. She was resplendent. A deep plunge cradled her not inconsiderable bosom, a fitting shelf for the diamonds that she placed there. Chandeliers of diamonds and sapphires cascaded from her ears and the look was completed by a cuff of the same jewels about her right wrist. She too was now ready. Together aunt and niece proceeded to the hotel dining room, festive in its trimmings of silver and blue.

For Sylvie the dinner passed in a whirl: the oysters unnoticed, the foie gras swallowed inattentively, the majestic roast turkey sending up its rich odours in vain. All her being was focused on the ball to come. Just as her impatience was becoming unbearable, the sound of violins tuning up announced that the dance was about to begin. From her seat at the table, Sylvie watched as the doors to the ballroom were flung open. With studied dignity the diners rose, abandoned their coffee cups and *digestifs* and made their way across the narrow hallway.

What was, in the day-to-day, the conference room, was now unrecognisable. Gone were the vinyl and tubular steel chairs, the individual desks, the lectern, the whiteboard. Gone was the serviceable brown nylon carpet with its inevitable stains of spilt coffee and insufficiently wiped shoes. A polished expanse of oak gleamed softly under the chandeliers. Little gold chairs upholstered in red velvet lined the walls. On the dais at the end of the room sat the string quartet, the men in full evening dress, the cellist in a white satin ruffled blouse and a wide, modesty-preserving skirt of black velvet. A subtle scent of vanilla and jasmine hung in the air and the first mellifluous strains of a waltz completed the transformation.

Halfway through the evening, the burglarious trio made their move. Jean-Luc and Jean-Marc had been observing the dancers closely.

'See that enormous woman in purple, with the pretty little girl at her heels?' said Jean-Marc. His twin nodded: he too had spotted, considered and calculated the value of the diamonds that glittered at the Marquise's throat, ears and wrists.

'I think this calls for the blind-sided switch, don't you?' he grinned.

Gaspard looked at him questioningly. Quickly the brothers outlined their plan, which brought a catch of glee to the country cousin's throat.

To him fell the task of distracting the niece, a task for which he felt more than ready.

As the string quartet paused for refreshment, a bevy of waiters circulated among the dancers, offering trays of champagne and canapes and cool moist towels to soothe the heat of their exertions. Turning to speak to Sylvie, Madame de Saint-Esprit was startled but not displeased to find at her elbow a tall, well-made young man in immaculate evening dress. Dark eyes caressed her face and figure as he bowed and introduced himself.

'Madame, I am Pierre de la Condamine, younger son of the Duc de Mersault whom you may see over there conversing with my mother. I would be most honoured if you would grant me the next dance.'

Sylvie, meanwhile, had her own admirer. Trying hard to look suave and nonchalant in a new midnight blue velvet dinner jacket, Gaspard had captured her hand and was murmuring in her ear. With her aunt distracted, Sylvie allowed herself to be led away onto the dance floor just as the musicians returned.

Jean-Luc, the supposed Pierre de la Condamine, had chosen his moment well. A discreetly folded 100-franc note had ensured that the next dance would be an up-tempo Viennese waltz. He was an accomplished dancer, and the Marquise found herself one minute whirled and flung to arm's length and the next clasped close as the young man – impudently but not disagreeably to the older woman – nuzzled at her shoulder, his fingers lightly caressing the nape of her neck.

The night was fine, though frosty, and the doors at the end of the long room had been opened onto a canopied terrace. The momentary cold was welcome as Jean-Luc expertly steered his partner out onto the candle-lit paving. The waltz finished with a tremendous flourish, and the young man whirled and twirled the Marquise into the shadows, momentarily letting go of her hand until, just at the last moment when she feared she would spin out of reach, he caught her hand again and brought her into a close embrace.

Laughing, breathless, the Marquise clasped her hand to her bosom, and shrieked.

'My diamonds! My diamonds have gone! What have you done with my diamonds?'

Sure enough, the opulent parure had disappeared from her throat, and her wrist was bare.

'I, Madame? Why, I have been with you this whole time. Is this some kind of a trick? Do you dare accuse me?' Indignation flashed in the black eyes that had smouldered so intimately into her own.

'Call the police,' demanded the Marquise.

The manager of the Hotel George V was summoned, and quickly alerted the authorities. Within a few minutes a young police officer, introducing himself as Bernard Durand, had appeared on the scene. Of course, the young man was questioned closely. Of course, it was soon established that no such person as the Duc de Mersault was present. This being the case, Durand had no hesitation in searching the impostor: his pockets, his shoes — even his underwear was not exempt. No diamonds were to be found, and the Marquise herself could attest that her partner had never for one moment left her side. A scam, Durand decided, but as to who was scamming whom, that was less certain. Bowing his apology he withdrew, promising to make further enquiries.

Provisionally exonerated, Jean-Luc melted into the crowd and was gone.

Back at their apartment, Jean-Luc and his twin brother howled with laughter.

'It works every time,' Jean-Marc cackled.

Dressed alike in sharply tailored evening dress, the twins were indistinguishable. Timing the moment to perfection, Jean-Marc had stepped in in the fraction of a second when his brother relinquished the Marquise's hand, allowing Jean-Luc to slip away with the jewels in his pocket and the lady none the wiser.

Gaspard had almost fallen at the first hurdle. His thick fingers had fumbled clumsily at the clasp of Sylvie's chain, causing her to gasp and start back. Luckily, an ardent kiss placed just at the corner of her mouth had swept away all alarm, and the necklace found its way safely into the apprentice thief's pocket. In the brouhaha of the Marquise's stolen diamonds, the sapphire was not missed for some time.

It was, if not a triumph for Gaspard, at least an auspicious beginning. Over the next few weeks, the three men carried out several more successful capers, though none as elaborate as the New Year's Eve scam. Gaspard was learning his trade, and with every operation his swagger grew. Soon he grew impatient under the twins' tutelage, confident that he could make his fortune alone. Jean-Luc and Jean-Marc held a private summit, after which they confronted their younger cousin.

'It's time for us to retire,' they announced. 'At least for the time being. We've done well, but there have been a few near-misses and that bastard Durand is getting closer. We are going to our parents' summer home at Carcassonne, and we advise you to take some time away from Paris as well, until the heat cools down.'

Gaspard was having none of it. He had learned a trick or two from his mentors, and a plan was forming in his head. A plan that involved an old but treasured enamel lapel pin, with the image of a small black cat...

So it was that Le Petit Chat was born.

In the spring of 1998, the hotel robberies began. Gaspard had learned one important lesson from his cousins: the trick of invisibility. As a concierge, a manager, a messenger, a delivering florist, a maintenance man — now in jeans and trainers, now in brown overalls, now in suit and tie — he slipped unobserved in and out of the grandest hotels, targeting only the wealthy and the powerful.

Wisely, he kept his success to himself. Others had come to grief, he knew, by ostentatiously splashing their ill-gotten cash. His base of operations remained the seedy hotel where he had first taken up residence; by day he was just another young man in jeans and a leather jacket, picking up work where he could, careful to pay his bills on time.

He travelled to Senlis, some 50km from Paris, and sought out an obscure print shop in a back street, where he commissioned the cards which would deliver his ironic message: on one side, the image of a black cat sitting on a wall; on the other, the words *Le Petit Chat vous remercie*. Months later the printer would read, in an old copy of *Le Parisien*, of the daring exploits of Le Petit Chat. He wondered, briefly, if he should tell what he knew, but the rich and famous were no friends of his and he shrugged and let it go.

Then came the affair of the singer's jewels, which brough near catastrophe to the budding burglar. *Le tout Paris* was talking about Lili La Voix, her great beauty. her extraordinary voice, the dazzling jewels she wore. Her three recitals at the Paris Olympe quickly sold out and tickets exchanged hands on the black market for thousands of francs. This, Gaspard decided, was to be his great coup, the jewel in his crown as it were. He smirked, congratulating himself on the pun.

It didn't go to plan. Yes, he slipped into Lili's bedroom in the darkest hours of the night. Yes, he made short work of the hotel safe and successfully abstracted the fabulous emeralds. But that was when it all went wrong.

Nobody could have been more astounded than Gaspard when, returning to his hotel the night after the emerald theft, he was confronted by Bernard Durand. Acting on instinct and panic he pushed the policeman away; Durand stumbled and fell, hitting his head against the cabin trunk where Gaspard kept his loot. Summoning the night porter, Gaspard bundled the unconscious Durand into the trunk and, sweating and cursing, the two men carried it downstairs and loaded it into the night porter's Renault van.

'Where shall we take him, Monsieur?' asked the porter.

Gaspard chuckled.

'Why, to the police station, of course,' he said.

The man looked at him aghast. Then a slow smile spread across his wrinkled features as Gaspard outlined his plan.

Two hours later, Gaspard was moving fast. It had been a close call, too close for comfort. The humiliated police officer would soon be on his trail. Paris had been a success but it was time to move on before he got caught.

With mixed emotions, Le Petit Chat turned his steps towards the south, and Morbignan la Crèbe.

Chapter 9:

REVELATIONS AT A PARTY

Morbignan La Crèbe, Saturday

Thierry was having none of it. Three of his most distinguished guests in a huddle with the most undesirable member of the party? This would not do. Turning the music up a little higher, he strode over to where Peitavy and Petit stood in a glowering head-to-head, while Durand and Richard Patterson looked on.

'*Allons, mes amis,*' he cajoled them. '*Venez danser.*'

Gaspard scoffed. 'Dance? I have no intention of dancing.' And with that he slumped once again into the armchair he had vacated.

Durand demurred. 'I'm sorry, Thierry, but I'm not up to any more capers. My knee is telling me it's time to sit down.'

Patterson noticed for the first time the walking stick with its elegantly curved handle which leant against his friend's chair. Nearing the end of what turned out to be an illustrious career, Durand had caught a stray bullet in his knee while preventing a bank robbery. The stick had been a retirement present from his colleagues. Durand normally used it more as an accessory than a necessity, but there were times when he was glad of its support.

Peitavy, on the other hand, didn't need to be asked twice. The music had set his toes tapping and soon he was off round the room again in a wild fandango of his own devising until, with an "*ouf!*", he sat down again with a thump and fanned himself with his hand. Beads of sweat glistened in his moustache.

'I'm getting too old for this kind of tomfoolery,' he complained to Henry Prendergast, who sat nursing a *petit blanc* and watching the proceedings with a certain amount of bewilderment. Henry's wife

164

Jeannette, perched on the arm of his chair, laughed with the elderly ex-*notaire.*

'I'm afraid my husband hasn't quite got the hang of village celebrations,' she said. Her father, Gaston, was dancing an excited polka round the room with his new wife, Marie Claire.

Henry leaned across.

'I was at the talk in the *Salle des Fêtes* yesterday. The atmosphere was amazing, that author really had the audience in the palm of her hand. She must be a very funny writer, judging by the huge amount of laughter going on all around me. I'm only sorry my French wasn't quite up to understanding all of it.'

Peitavy tapped the side of his nose.

'Well, now, I'm going to let you into a little secret…' he began, but he was interrupted by a huge cheer. Underneath the music and the hubbub of the party, Céleste had detected a discreet knock at the door and had rushed to open it for their distinguished guest.

Ysabel had dressed for the occasion: her cream silk skirt fell in soft folds to her ankles, cinched by a wide scarlet leather belt. The shawl about her shoulders was splashed with scarlet poppies, and long earrings of the same colour brushed the shoulders of her silk blouse. A strikingly pretty young woman with long auburn hair had slipped in behind Ysabel, almost unnoticed, and stood smiling shyly at the gathering.

At once Ysabel was engulfed in a tide of exclamations and compliments – everyone wanted a word with the celebrated writer. Disengaging herself with smiles and polite murmurs, she went up to Thierry; kissing him three times on the cheeks in Languedoc fashion she presented him with her gifts: a signed set of her books and a box of fine cigars.

'*Bon anniversaire,* Thierry,' she congratulated her host.

She turned to where Peitavy had risen to his feet, bursting with pride.

'*Bonsoir Papa,*' she said and embraced him. Some of the party guests gasped, others exchanged 'I knew it all along' smiles.

'It is true.' Peitavy swelled like a turkey cock, the ends of his moustache quivering with delight.

'Mesdames, Messieurs, I have the honour to present to you my daughter, Isabelle, better known to many of you as the celebrated author Ysabel de la Fontaine.

'And here,' he held out his hand and the younger woman came forward. 'Here is my beautiful grand-daughter, Mademoiselle Bienvenue de la Fontaine.'

165

'Luckily for her – and for me,' Peitavy continued over the babble of voices, 'Bienvenue is nothing like her father.' The room fell silent; expectant eyes turned towards the former *notaire*.

'It is no honour to me,' he went on, 'to present to you the disreputable lout whom I have the great good fortune *not* to call my son in law. This despicable *voyou* once took advantage of the naïve affections of my innocent daughter. Then, leaving her shamed and heartbroken once he had had his way, he married another woman and then skulked off to Paris and got up to who knows what villainy. I can only applaud Isabelle for her determination and courage in making a new life for herself and for her lovely daughter.

'Perhaps you would care to know the identity of this *sale type*?' Heads nodded vigorously, eyes widened with expectation. 'Very well than. Step forward, brave and honourable... Gaspard Petit.'

'*Salaud!* You bastard!' A small, feisty woman who had been sitting quietly chatting to Céleste launched herself at Gaspard and delivered two resounding slaps to his face. It was Mireille Petit.

'You despicable son of a syphilitic camel,' she spat at her husband.

'Was it not enough to deceive me, to marry me for my father's money and then to run away when he expected you to work for it? That betrayal was bad, but this is far worse. Isabelle was a child when you left, you disgusting bastard. You seduced her and then dumped her when she told you she was pregnant. And then you came crawling back when whatever you were up to in Paris went sour.

'I am the fool in all this,' she went on, turning to the partygoers who were lapping up the scene with a mixture of fascination and horror.

'I took him back, when I should have kicked him out of the door the moment he showed his ugly face back in Morbignan.

'My dear, I am so sorry,' she said, addressing Ysabel. 'None of us had any idea what had happened to you, or who was responsible. If I'd known, I'd have gone to Paris myself and dragged his sorry backside here and made him make amends. Forgive me.'

Ysabel embraced her. 'There is nothing to forgive. You were young too, then. And we both know just how charming Gaspard could be, back in the day. I have had my revenge – yours is still to come.'

Mireille smiled. 'Yes, I have my own story,' she conceded. 'And as for revenge... well, we shall see.'

Chapter 10:

GASPARD AND THE WIFE

Morbignan La Crèbe 1998

It wasn't the triumphant return Gaspard had envisaged. He'd seen himself arriving in splendour, wealthy beyond the dreams of avarice, to fill the villagers with awe and show that cretin of a father-in-law what a splendid husband his daughter Mimi had managed to capture.

If the truth be told, he hadn't imagined returning to Morbignan at all. Oh yes, he would have passed through like a shooting star, trailing clouds of glory, but his sights were set on new horizons, new triumphs.

But now, with Durand seeking him in Paris and nowhere else to go now that his cousins had retired, Morbignan seemed a useful temporary refuge. He grinned to himself at the thought of the policeman desperately trying to track him down in the capital, while all the time he, Gaspard Petit, was back in the village right under Durand's nose, so to speak.

And here was Mimi, waiting for him, although not exactly with open arms. Mimi. It was all her fault. She was supposed to be The One: not the love of his life but, far more importantly, his passport to a life of leisure and comfort. If Mimi and, especially, her *salaud* of a father, had been more amenable, things would have been very different.

Three years earlier

It had started well enough, Gaspard remembered. Mireille – or Mimi as everyone called her – was a newcomer to the Lycée where he now worked as a caretaker. By this time, he had grown into his physique: he was almost half a metre taller than the boy mocked by his schoolmates for his attempts at a moustache. His broad shoulders, narrow waist and snake hips gave full value to his wardrobe, purchased from the most stylish of the *friperies* (second-hand clothes stalls) in the market in St

167

Rémy. Carefully cultivated sideburns complemented the moustache, still in place but now shaped and groomed to perfection.

In *première* (Year 12), just at the time when teenage boys were beginning to realise that girls weren't so stupid after all, Mimi had exploded into the classroom. She had begun her studies in Paris, under the watchful eye of an aunt, but certain rumours had reached her family, causing her father to recall her to the village school to do her *Baccalauréat* in less exciting surroundings.

With her dancing green eyes, anarchic sense of humour and fashionable clothes, Mimi took the class by storm. All the boys wanted to go out with her, all the girls wanted to be her.

Gaspard played it cool. Confident in his looks, he knew that being older, an adult, gave him a considerable advantage over the puppyish students who fawned on Mimi. Biding his time, he took extra care with his hair and clothes; his fingernails were clean and a ghost of Brut followed him down the school corridors.

He realised that Mimi was used to being pursued; in fact, she expected it. As the boys in her class followed her around with stars in their eyes, Gaspard could see her casting surreptitious glances over to where he was engrossed in something other than her. Sometimes he would allow her to catch his eye, and he would smile and bow slightly and then go back to what he was doing. He could tell it infuriated her. More and more, he noticed, she was finding ways of crossing his path, always with downcast eyes and a *moue* as if of disdain. He wasn't fooled.

'She will be mine,' he boasted to his cronies in *L'Estaminet*. 'It's just a matter of time: I will let her chase me until I catch her.' It was probably the only witty thing he ever said.

It was *Le Quatorze* that presented him with his opportunity. The July 14th Bastille Day celebrations were a communal affair in Morbignan. Trestle tables were set up in the square and the whole village congregated to eat *moules marinières* and *brochettes de veau* and drink as much of the famous local Château Rouge-Gorge as they could consume. There was music and dancing, and the highlight of the evening was a spectacular firework display.

Mimi's family were all there: the wealthy *vigneron* Jean-Jacques Depardieu, accompanied by the 17-year-old Mireille, her younger sister Florence and his wife Dulcinée. Mimi's little dog, Bambou, trotted happily at their heels, his bright eyes never missing an opportunity to snatch a morsel from an unwary diner's plate.

Bambou was quite blasé about fireworks: distant bangs and crackles held no terror for him. But, unbeknown to the Depardieu family and most of the villagers, the fête committee had decided to mix things up a little this year. Instead of holding the display down by the river, nearly half a kilometre away from the village square, they had decided to let off the fireworks *sur place*, in a cordoned-off area which most people had supposed to be reserved for the musicians.

An ear-splitting bang announced the start of the fireworks display, followed by the loud crackle of cascading stars in blue and green and silver. Bambou almost jumped out of his skin and hit the ground running. Before Mimi could grab him, he had rounded the corner of the *boulangerie* and disappeared into the dark labyrinth of streets in the oldest part of the village.

Gaspard, who had been leaning against the bench under the plane tree, seemingly engrossed in conversation with his cronies, had been keeping a speculative eye on Mireille's family. Scarcely had Mimi dissolved into tears in the comforting arms of her mother, than Gaspard was away. He hared off in pursuit of the little dog, his ears attuned to the terrified scrabble of paws on cobbled streets. It wasn't long before he found Bambou, huddled shivering in a doorway; he scooped him up and brought him back in triumph to his mistress. Mimi's thanks were all that he could have wished for. As he kissed her cheek and took her hand to lead her to the dance area, *maman* and *papa* looked on approvingly.

Soon the news was all over the Lycée: Mireille had found herself a handsome boyfriend, a grown-up with a motorbike and money to spend. The boys were in despair, the girls consumed with envy.

Gaspard played his cards cleverly: this was no passing fancy, to love and leave. Mimi was the girl he would marry. He knew her father was rich in acres of supremely productive vineyard and also owned a lucrative wine bottling business. Mimi, as his elder daughter, would one day be a wealthy heiress; in the meantime, Gaspard could see a cushy life for himself running Papa's thriving enterprises.

The couple settled into a steady courtship. Gaspard was careful to keep Mimi on side, unaware – or so he thought – of his occasional peccadilloes. After all, he reasoned to himself, he would be doing her a great favour by marrying her, and a man was entitled to the occasional dalliance.

Mimi didn't quite see it that way. Yes, Gaspard was handsome and pleasing, but he was by no means the only string to her bow. If he proved unsatisfactory there were others who would step in, only too pleased to squire the prettiest and most popular girl in the village and, furthermore, the girl blessed with the rich papa. If Mimi had known about her boyfriend's affair with Isabelle, she would have shrugged her pretty shoulders and laughed. Gaspard was hers, until she decided otherwise.

They announced their engagement on Mireille's 19th birthday and married the following year. When, days before the wedding, Isabelle had come to Gaspard in tears, confessing her pregnancy, he had laughed at her. On the day the devastated girl fled to Paris, Gaspard and Mireille stood before the *maire* and made their vows.

If Gaspard expected it all to be plain sailing, now that he had captured his prize, he was in for a rude awakening. On the morning after the couple arrived back from honeymoon, Gaspard strolled nonchalantly into Jean-Jacques' office.

'Now, papa,' he began cheekily, 'what have you got for me?'

Jean-Jacques regarded his son-in-law with a baleful eye. He had the measure of this young man. Yes, he was Mimi's choice, and as a doting father he wanted nothing more than his daughter's happiness. But the young whelp was a trifle too cocky for his liking and needed to be taken down a peg.

'Welcome to the family, my son,' he began. 'I am not so young as I was, and it is good to have a strapping young man to shoulder some of the burdens of my many enterprises.'

Gaspard smiled, smugly: this was going to plan.

'I take it you know nothing of the wine business?'

Gaspard shook his head.

'Well, *tant pis*, I am sure you will soon learn. First of all, you should spend a few months in the vines with my foreman, Gui. He will show you how we weed and prune the plants to get them ready for the fruit bearing season. There is quite a lot of work at this time of year, but I am sure you won't mind that. Then, of course, there is the *vendange,* the harvest. We do bring in some casual labour to help, but the family does the main part of the work.'

Gaspard was looking at his father-in-law with disbelief.

'What? You expect me to work in the vines like a common *paysan*? Me, who married your daughter not three weeks ago?'

The vigneron regarded him calmly.

'Of course, what did you expect? Did you think I was just going to hand over the reins to you, when you know nothing of the business?

You'll learn your trade first, my lad, before there's any talk of management.'

That evening, Gaspard and Mimi had their first serious row. He stormed into their cottage full of indignation and poured out his tale of outrage.

'And worst of all,' he concluded, 'your *sacré papa* expects me to labour in the vines, as if I weren't your husband and a valued member of the family.'

Mimi looked at him placidly over the cassoulet she was preparing.

'*Eh bien*? Why are you so surprised? This is a working family. What made you think things would be any different for you?

'Well, if that's what you and your precious papa think, you can just think again.'

Gaspard stormed out of the house and went to sleep at his friend Lucien's house. Lucien was all sympathy and indignation.

'How dare they treat you this way?' he exclaimed. 'Doesn't Mimi know what a catch you were? Doesn't Jean-Jacques realise what a valuable asset you could be?'

'Well, it's their loss.' Suddenly, Gaspard made up his mind. 'I'm not staying here to be disrespected like this. My cousins have been begging me to join them in Paris – they have a very nice little business going there. I'm not sure exactly what it is, but I know they make a lot of money. I'm going to have me some of that, and Mireille and her family can go to hell.'

Used to his friend's outbursts, Lucien nodded encouragingly. There was no way that Gaspard, however big a fish he was in the small pond of Morbignan, would venture to the big city.

Yet, three days later, Gaspard was gone.

Chapter 11:

ROBBED OF HIS BIG MOMENT

Morbignan la Crèbe, Saturday

Gaspard was fuming. That oaf of a *notaire* had made a fool of him. He had been planning to make his own announcement: the moment Ysbabel made her entrance he had seen an opportunity. He could hear himself:

'Welcome, *ma belle*,' he would cry. 'How proud I am that my little village girlfriend has made such a glittering career for herself.

'Oh, yes,' he would continue proudly as the jaws of the gathering dropped. 'I have been following her triumph for years, and I am delighted that, in my own modest way, I have contributed to it. Yes, indeed: *Glou-glou, c'est moi*! I am Glou-glou!'

Here he would pause for the applause and congratulations that he knew would come his way. And then, with a deprecating cough, he would continue:

'And how overjoyed I am to see my beautiful daughter here today. You can tell, can you not, how she takes after her Papa in beauty and charm?'

None of it had gone to plan. It was Peitavy, the stupid bumpkin with his absurd moustaches, who had made the announcement. It was Peitavy who received the plaudits that Gaspard knew were his due. And then, to cap it all, his own wife had humiliated him, slapping his face in public like that.

With a growl he launched himself at Mimi, hands grasping for her throat. He would end this charade once and for all.

'Now, now, NOW!' Someone grasped his arm and a peremptory voice rang out. 'I've told you about that kind of thing before, have I not?'

Gaspard blinked. There before him, arms akimbo, stood a stocky Englishwoman, as wide as she was tall and with a belligerent scowl on her face.

'You!' he bellowed, face crimson. 'You are the mother of that *sale métisse*, the filthy half-breed of who knows what paternity. Ever since your accursed family moved into the house next door to me you have gone out of your way to make my life a misery.'

Betty Brayford regarded him calmly. Her French wasn't yet fluent enough to make out her neighbour's words, but the tone was unmistakeable. Still holding Gaspard's arm in a firm grip, she squared up to him.

'Now listen here,' she said slowly. 'You are a bully and an oaf. I've been watching your behaviour and, trust me, it leaves a lot to be desired. If my Larry were here, God rest his soul, he'd have a thing or two to say about it, you mark my words. But don't fool yourself that just 'cos I'm a woman I don't know how to deal with yobs like you.'

She could see it was wasted on him: he was barely competent in his own language, let alone in English.

'In other words, my lad...' she took a deep breath, than proudly produced the sentence she had learned only a week ago. If the accent was atrocious, the words were nonetheless clear.

'*Va... te... faire... foutre!*'

There was a collective gasp, then a storm of cheers and applause for the valiant little Englishwoman. Mimi burst into laughter, repeating:

'*Oui, mon cher,* do as the nice English lady tells you: *va te faire foutre!*'

'Enough!' Gaspard bellowed. Furious, humiliated, he pushed Bettty aside and stormed out of the door.

No-one noticed who slipped out behind him.

Still chuckling, Betty walked over to where her daughter Alex and son-in-law James were chatting to Richard Patterson. Henry Prendergast joined them.

'I say,' he said, 'did that mean what I thought it meant?'

'It most certainly did,' she answered with a smile. 'Get stuffed. Only it's a bit ruder in French. And it's thanks to my charming neighbour that I learned how to say it in French.

'I take it you have had a run-in or two with Gaspard Petit,' said Patterson. 'He's the bane of all our lives, in a way, but mostly he is too drunk to be any real problem. And he's the biggest coward: if you face up to him, he soon backs down.

'He turned up on our doorstep once, drunk as a skunk and ranting some nonsense about the Queen of England. Martha opened the door to him, and her French is a lot better than mine, but she just stood there and laughed at him. Howled with laughter, in fact. The more he threatened the more she laughed, until he finally gave up and went away. He hasn't given us any trouble since.'

'Unfortunately, he is our next-door neighbour,' James Carcenet said. 'We'd hardly moved in before he started acting up.'

Chapter 12:

GASPARD AND THE NEW NEIGHBOURS

Morbignan la Crèbe, one year earlier

'Oh for heaven's sake, James, let me do it!' Betty swung the cardboard box onto her shoulder and strode off in the direction of the studio. James Carcenet gazed at his mother-in-law with a mixture of affection and exasperation. Approaching her 70th year hadn't slowed Betty down, nor had it softened her acerbic tongue.

Would it work? He gazed round the kitchen, its red-flagged floor almost invisible under boxes and carrier bags and a heap of coats, shoes and a solitary slipper.

Alex puffed up the front steps, grinning, her curly black hair glinting with sweat.

'Hot, isn't it?' she signed, waving her hand in front of her face.

James' heart lifted. Of course it would work, he told himself. He and Alex would make a home of this rambling old village farmhouse, with its two-foot-thick walls and tiled floors. Betty, independent as always, would nest in what they had christened the studio, a stone-built barn facing the house across a small courtyard. Already P'tit Gui and his workmen had been into the studio, setting a proper frame in the ragged hole which passed for a window and shoring up the teetering staircase.

'Time for a cuppa.' Betty was back. She had unearthed a kettle and a box of tea bags from the chaos.

'Tea?' queried Alex, 'in this heat?'

Betty turned to face her daughter. 'Best thing in the world to cool you down,' she said distinctly. 'If there's one thing your good-for-nothing father taught me it was that. And he knew a thing or two about heat.'

Alex laughed. Growing up, she had never tired of hearing tales of Deaf Larry, her glamorous, villainous dad, and his East-end crew. Ask Larry where he came from and he'd say 'Hoxton,' with a stare that

175

challenged you to question him, but his dark skin and dark-treacle accent hinted at origins much further south and east.

Betty went to plug in the kettle and stopped.

'Oh, dear.' She looked in dismay from the three-pin English plug to the two-hole French socket.

'I think this is what you're looking for.' Handing her an adapter, James smiled to himself. He knew that Betty regarded him as something of a wimp. About as useful as a chocolate teapot, as she would say. After all, a mild-mannered antiquarian bookseller had come as a bit of a surprise after the previous boyfriends Alex had brought home.

'I have my uses,' James thought to himself, as Betty busied herself making tea.

'Let's walk over to the bar later,' he suggested. 'Get to know a few people.'

The Carcenet family were by no means the first English people to settle in Morbignan la Crèbe. Henry Prendergast – forever dubbed *l'anglais'* – and the poet Richard Patterson had made their niche in the little community. They and their wives shopped conscientiously in the *épicerie* and the *boulangerie*, said *bonjour* politely when they encountered a neighbour, swept their front steps and stood in line like everyone else, of a Thursday evening, for one of the aromatic pizzas cooked up by Jo-Jo in his little catering van.

After much consideration, the villagers had decided they were *des gens correctes* – OK people - and welcomed them into their midst. Subject to approval, they were ready to extend the same courtesy to James, Alex and Betty. True, Alex's spectacular good looks and caramel skin had raised a few eyebrows when Jean-Jacques the estate agent had first brought them to view the house. Luckily, Betty's warm, no-nonsense approach and optimistic attempts at French had soon melted some of the frost.

'By the way,' Betty said, pouring tea, 'I've already met one of the neighbours. That is, I've seen him. He was at the window of the house just across the way. He seemed friendly enough at first: he grinned at me. But when I tried saying *bonjour, Monsieur'* – James winced – 'he just shrugged and turned away.'

Next door, Gaspard Petit was lurking at the window of his kitchen, the only room that overlooked the Carcenets' house. He held a half-full bottle of *rosé* in his fist and glowered through the gap in the shutters.

'Some people have moved into that Dubosc woman's house,' he muttered. 'They're English, and one of them's black. *Sales anglais, sale métisse*,' he spat.

Mimi went on chopping onions, ignoring her husband. Gaspard took another big glug of wine and stormed out of the kitchen.

'Call me when dinner's ready,' he ordered.

Later that evening, James and his family strolled across the little village square towards the café. Half a dozen of the local good ol' boys were sitting on the circular bench under the plane tree; they greeted the newcomers with much doffing of caps and waving of canes. Their ancient eyes lit up with approval at Alex's skin-tight jeans and skimpy top, and they accorded her a special '*Bonsoir, Madame*,' twinkling at her benevolently. Alex waved cheerfully and James gave a half-bow, mustering his best '*Bonsoir, Messieurs.*'

Conversation stopped abruptly in *l'Estaminet* as they walked into the café. Glasses of beer halted mid-way to lips and heads swivelled to inspect the newcomers. The café's owner, Marie Claire, came out from behind the bar to greet them.

'*Soir, m'sieur-dames.*' she said, then, screwing up her face with the effort, she added 'Good eevenink, sir and ladies.'

They found a shady table on the terrace and Marie Claire brought out their drinks: a pastis for James, a coffee for Betty and for Alex a newly discovered *diabolo menthe* – iced lemonade with a dash of mint syrup. Marie Claire paused to smile at the younger woman, signing energetically to her mother, then turned and headed for a table inside the café. A moment later, a tall, distinguished-looking man approached the Carcenets' table.

'Good evening, I'm Richard Patterson,' he introduced himself, as his fingers repeated the same message.

'James Carcenet,' said James, surprised, 'my wife Alex and her mother, Betty. You sign?'

'Yes, my brother is profoundly deaf, and we all learned together as children.'

Alex's fingers were busy again and James frowned.

'Sitting on a bench?' he queried. 'I don't understand.'

Alex nodded, smiling up at the Englishman.

Patterson laughed, colouring slightly.

'Aha, do I detect a fan?'

Seeing the blank look on James' face he explained,

'I'm a poet. Well, I wouldn't go that far: more of a versifier, really. I wrote a parody of that Lewis Carroll poem – you know, the white knight, "sitting on a gate". Mine is "sitting on a bench," which by happy coincidence is a perfect rhyme for French. It's dedicated to our local good ol' boys – whom I gather you've met,' he added with a laugh.

'The poem had some small success back home in England, and people always seem to greet me with those words.'

James apologised. 'I'm so sorry, my interest has always been in old books and old texts. I'm not really up to date with modern writing. Alex is the reader in the family.'

A round, dimpled woman wandered over to join them.

'I'm Martha,' she said, tucking her hand into the crook of Patterson's arm. 'And I have the great good fortune to be wife to this lofty lump of oddity. You must be the people who have moved into Héloïse Dubosc's house on the *rue de l'église*. We live just round the corner in the *chemin du barrage*.'

'Woof,' said a small brown and white head, peering round Martha's legs.

'Oh, I beg your pardon,' Martha said, bending to ruffle the dog's ears. 'I didn't introduce the most important member of the family. This is Visitor.'

'B and B might question your use of the words "most important",' grumbled Patterson.

Alex had been following the conversation carefully. Now she looked confused.

'B&B?' she signed. 'Bed and breakfast?'

'Oh, sorry, I should have explained. We have two black and white cats, too, brothers called Banjax and Bandicoot.' Richard Patterson signed the names carefully, letter by letter, and Alex burst out laughing.

'Yes, I know, rather outlandish names. You can blame Martha for that. She names everything! And when we got the boys she told me that ever since she was a small child she'd wanted two black and white cats called Banjax and Bandicoot. So there you are.'

'And Visitor?' Alex wanted to know.

'Ah, thereby hangs a tale. For about a year she would turn up at our house from time to time, so we called her Visitor. Then she sort of became ours, as nobody seemed to own her, and the name stuck.'

The little dog in question, meanwhile, had made herself comfortable on Alex's lap.

'Would you care to join us,' James said, 'as your dog appears to have done so already.'

As they seated themselves and James ordered another round of drinks, Betty said, 'Everybody in the village is very friendly, so far. But we do have a rather peculiar neighbour.'

Richard and his wife exchanged glances.

'I saw him at his window,' Betty continued. 'He grinned at me, so I said '*bonjour monsieur*' very politely, and the next thing I knew he'd slammed the shutters closed.'

'The grin is meant to terrify you,' Martha said, grinning herself. 'That's old Gaspard Petit. We call him Cat Little. He was a kind of burglar in Paris, many years ago, called himself Le Petit Chat – the little cat. You ask our friend Durand: he was a copper in Paris at the time. He'll have a thing or two to tell you about Petit.

'The man hates everyone, especially the English. He's quite meek if you stand up to him, especially if he isn't full of *rosé*, but there have been one or two nasty incidents, so watch out for him.'

Betty snorted.

'Nasty incidents? I've handled a few of those in my time and no little turd of a Frenchman – 'scuse my French – is going to give me or my family grief.'

Looking at her belligerent jaw and the steely spark in her eyes, Martha could well believe it.

The Carcenets settled in almost seamlessly. The villagers were, on the whole, well-disposed to the English in Morbignan la Crèbe, especially those who were prepared to buy up the old and rather inconvenient stone-built houses and live in them. Holidaymakers they viewed with scorn and the Parisians, of course, they hated, as any right-minded Languedocian would.

Gaspard Petit kept a low profile, confining himself to the occasional oath hurled from his kitchen window. His wife, Mimi, would smile at them in the street but declined to stop for a chat. As the hot days continued and, like everyone else not blessed with *le clim'* (air conditioning), the Carcenets kept their shutters closed and windows open day and night, they often found the gentle night sounds of roosting swifts and hunting barn owls interrupted by the less than dulcet tones of Gaspard ranting at the world. Sometimes Mimi's voice could be heard, attempting to soothe him, but more often than not she stayed silent while her husband roared.

'Do you think she's afraid of him?' Alex wondered.

Betty sniffed. 'Not in this universe,' she said. 'That girl's got a spark in her eye. Strikes me, she's just biding her time.'

Mimi could indeed hold her own: it was her very feistiness that precipitated the first round of what was to be an ongoing battle between Gaspard and the Carcenets. It was a Wednesday, and Betty was returning from the weekly market in the *place du marché*. She had gone to buy potatoes and onions and one of the delicious *daubes* dished up by the visiting deli from St Laurent: Maison Dupuy. Instead, Betty had encountered Tiphaine, on one of her occasional visits to the village market, and all thoughts of food had flown out of her head.

Tiphaine was the local *antiquaire,* her stall piled high with questionable antiques: worm-eaten milking stools, chipped bowls, corroded 'solid copper' pans, lurching standard lamps, collectable coffee tins – anything to set the eyes of the holiday-homers a-gleam. She had made it her business to acquire a fluent, if idiosyncratic, command of the English language, and she made a nice living doing the round of the villages where the prosecco set had their *maisons secondaires*.

Something in the heap of rubbish had caught Betty's eye.

'Is that a thing for smoking meat?' she said, holding the object aloft. Rusty and cobwebbed, it was a set of four deep iron hooks joined in the centre to form something like an upturned hand.

'It's a *crémaillère,*' said Tiphaine. 'You hang it in your chimney to suspend your *marmite*, your pot, when cooking. You hear French people say *pendre la crémaillère*, it means warming the new house. A party.'

Betty wasn't listening. Whatever the thing was, and whatever it had to do with parties was irrelevant. A touch of wire brush, a touch of Hammerite and she could just see it hanging in an alcove in her kitchen with aromatic bunches of herbs dangling from its four arms.

'How much?' she enquired.

Five minutes later she was hurrying home clutching her prize, for which she had paid considerably less than Tiphaine had asked, and a tad more than Tiphaine had hoped to get. Such is the way of market transactions.

Raised voices alerted her as she turned up the *rue de l'église*. Gaspard, well-fuelled with *rosé*, was laying down the law at the top of his voice. Mimi, facing him with fists on her hips, was unimpressed, and her voice matched his in volume. Sensing a run-of-the-mill domestic, Betty was about to take a tactful detour when Gaspard lunged at his much smaller wife and shook her roughly by the arm.

'Here, here, we're having none of that,' Betty said, marching up to the couple.

Gaspard's piggy eyes popped with astonishment: was this diminutive Englishwoman daring to challenge him? He raised his fist and swung. Almost casually, Betty caught the fist in flight and, stepping back, used his own momentum to send him sprawling.

'Now,' she said sweetly, 'piss off and behave yourself, or you'll have me to deal with.' And as Gaspard lurched to his feet, muttering threats, she helped him on his way with a tap on the backside from her size 7 Doc Martins.

'Brave as a lion, that one,' she remarked. 'The cowardly lion from the Wizard of Oz, that is.'

Mimi was shaking, tears running down her face.

'Bravo!' she said, choking on laughter, '*C'est bien fait*! (well done).' And, revealing a surprising command of English, she added: 'One of zese days I will keel zat man.'

'What is the matter with that man?' James enquired a few days later, as he and Richard Patterson shared a pre-dinner pastis in the café.

'Is it the English in general he hates, or have I done something to offend him?'

'I think your ma-in-law may have had something to do with it,' said Patterson. 'Old Madame Meunière just happened to be looking out of her window and she saw the whole thing. You know what a gossip she is: by the next morning the whole village was laughing. Petit walked into the bar yesterday and someone shouted, '*Attention à la grandmère!*' (Watch out for the granny!) and everyone fell about.

'But the truth is, he hates all foreigners, and the ironic thing is, he isn't even French: he's Portuguese, at least on his mother's side. Nobody in the village has much time for him, and how that lovely wife of his puts up with him I do not know. She could do a lot better.'

At first, Gaspard Petit was nothing but a source of innocent merriment to the Carcenets. When he grinned from his window, whoever was in the courtyard would grin back. When he shook his fist, they waved amicably. When he pursued them in the street shouting '*Sales anglais*, go home to your Queen Elizabeth' they laughed and offered to shake hands.

Things were a little less funny when he took to pursuing Alex if she went out alone. He would mimic her signing with obscene gestures or creep up behind her and pounce, grabbing her arm or jumping in front of her making monkey faces.

Alex was her mother's daughter, not easily intimidated, but James grew increasingly angry.

'Someone needs to put a stop to that drunken bully,' he remarked more than once, 'and if no-one else does, I will.'

'You're right,' said his mother-in-law thoughtfully. Sooner or later, something will have to be done.'

Chapter 13

INCROYABLE!

Morbignan La Crèbe, Saturday

'Well, that was a bit of entertainment Céleste hadn't planned,' Richard Patterson laughed as Gaspard Petit departed and the ruckus died away. 'He really is an awful lout, that man. '

'But what I don't understand,' he went on, 'is how Ysabel got him so bang to rights. According to Martha he's exactly like the fat oaf she describes in her books, but surely when Ysabel knew him he was young and apparently quite handsome.'

James Carcenet leaned forward. 'Oh, I can answer that one,' he said. 'I had quite a chat with her the other night, after the signing. She speaks surprisingly good English, by the way. I told her about our experiences with Petit and after she'd finished laughing she promised faithfully not to put them in her next book, but I'm not convinced.

'Anyway, it seems she kept in touch with happenings in Morbignan. She contacted her parents soon after the baby was born; they've been to Paris to see her a few times and they talk on the phone and exchange emails all the time. When she started writing the Glou-glou books, Peitavy used to tell her all about Gaspard. He even managed to get a photo of him once: he was taking photographs of the *Foire de Morbignan*, the spring fair, and Petit just happened to walk by.

'She saw him, you know,' Carcenet continued.

'Who saw who?' said Richard, somewhat ungrammatically.

'Ysabel saw Gaspard. It was in the early days, just after he came to Paris. That hotel that Durand found him in, it was in the *sixième arrondissement*, just a couple of streets away from her first apartment. She said he was wearing a flashy suit and he looked like a cut price Mafioso. Needless to say, she did not speak to him.'

'Do you suppose she knew then just what a *voyou* he really was?' Henry Prendergast wondered, proud of his use of the newly acquired term.

'I mean, we've all had a laugh at his expense, and some of us have had our problems, but who knew, until Durand told us, that he was the glamorous jewel thief they called Le Petit Chat?'

'Excuse me?' An elegantly dressed, grey-haired woman had been standing unnoticed behind Alex Carcenet's chair. Now she edged forward.

'Forgive me for interrupting, but I couldn't help overhearing what you said. That fat man, the one who was making all that noise, that's Gaspard Petit, yes? And you say he was Le Petit Chat? *Incroyable!*'

Patterson laughed.

'It's certainly *incroyable* to look at him today but, yes, he had a brief career as a jewel thief in Paris some decades ago. Our friend Durand, the policeman, very nearly caught him once. It's a good story, you must get him to tell it to you some day. He actually met his wife through Petit: he recovered her emeralds which Le Petit Chat had stolen. But I imagine from your reaction that you have your own story to tell.'

The woman smiled. 'Of course, where are my manners? I should have introduced myself. My name is Sylvie Thornfield, but I was Sylvie de Lacoste when I had the misfortune to come across that man. I was in Paris for my first big *bal de réveillon*, that's the New Year's Eve ball, at the Hotel George V.

'My aunt, the Marquise de Saint-Esprit, had invited me up to accompany her. It was my first time in Paris and I was very excited. When the ball started, an awful young man introduced himself as the son of the Duc de Mersault and invited my aunt to dance. At the end of the dance her wonderful diamonds were missing. Everyone was sure he had stolen them, but no-one could prove it. Of course, there was no Duc de Mersault present at the ball.'

Betty had been listening attentively. 'And Petit?' she prompted.

'Petit? Oh, you mean Le Petit Chat. Well, he asked me to dance while my aunt was dancing with the so-called Duke's son, and then I discovered my sapphire necklace was missing too. And so was the young man! I'm sure those two were working together; the police questioned everybody at the ball, but nobody knew anything.'

'But you said your name is now Sylvie Thornfield?' Betty asked. 'There's an Englishman in the village called Thornfield, is that a coincidence?'

She looked over to where a white-haired man, bulging out of his skinny jeans, was talking a little too intimately with Ysabel's daughter

Bienvenue. As Betty watched, Ysabel smoothly scooped the girl up on the pretext of introducing her to a neighbour.

Sylvie followed her glance.

'No, no coincidence,' she sighed. 'That's my husband, Robin. Soon to be my ex, though. Oddly enough I met him through Le Petit Chat as well.'

Chapter 14:

AN INGLORIOUS RETURN

Morbignan la Crèbe 1998

'He still isn't too bad looking, in a *louche* kind of way,' Mireille Petit said to herself. 'I suppose I could do worse.'

That shock of white hair above a youngish face certainly made him striking, she reflected. That is, until you noticed the soft sag under the chin, the pinkness about the eyes, the burgeoning *embonpoint* straining the buttons of his faded denim shirt.

Robin Thornfield fancied himself as Jack-the-Lad in the little village of Morbignan la Crèbe. He and Mireille had had a mild fling some years earlier, while she was still studying for her *Baccalauréat*. Confident in her looks and sex-appeal, Mireille had played the field with enthusiasm, all the while keeping a surreptitious eye on Gaspard Petit, who was proving a more difficult fish to land.

Mireille giggled to herself as she remembered the day Gaspard had finally proposed. She and Robin had snatched a few romantic moments while Gaspard was supposedly working. When he suddenly burst into the bar and strode up to the secluded corner where the guilty couple were snuggling, it almost came to blows. The fight, of course, was all bluff and bluster: two dyed-in-the-wool cowards batting at each other with outstretched arms like six-year-olds. Still, it caught Gaspard's attention, and two days later he asked her to marry him.

Since Gaspard's precipitous departure for Paris at the end of the previous year, Mireille hadn't lacked for company. Of all her admirers, Robin Thornfield was the most persistent. She was just debating whether to give in to his advances when, equally suddenly, her husband reappeared in Morbigan.

Mireille and Robin had met by arrangement in *L'Estaminet*. Just as Robin was returning from the bar with their drinks, who should slouch in but Gaspard Petit? Mireille gasped, raised her hand half in greeting, half in protest. Cutting straight across Thornfield, Gaspard swept Mireille up in his arms and gave her three hearty kisses on the cheeks before latching his mouth onto hers. Over his shoulder, Mimi's eyes signalled to Thornfield that now was the time to quit the scene.

'*Me voilà, ma belle, tu es contente de me revoir?*' ('Here I am, my beauty, aren't you glad to see me again?') he roared at full volume, and then:

'*Toi!*' he roared even louder, spotting Thornfield. 'You get away from my wife, you *saulaud*, or you won't be seducing the ladies when I have finished with you.'

Thornfield smiled and shrugged.

'Bah! What do I care for your wife?' he taunted. 'There are other fish in the sea, younger and prettier than your Mimi. I was just doing her a favour, keeping her company while you got up to god knows what in Paris.'

Inwardly, though, he was seething. Was Mimi going to ditch him for a village lout who obviously couldn't make it in Paris and who had come home with his tail between his legs? Never mind that he, Robin Thornfield, had enough female company and to spare. Never mind that he had a steady girlfriend safely tucked away in Les Herbes. Never mind that he had a 'wife' and two children in Clermont l'Hérault, whom he visited often enough to convince her that they were really married. None of this mattered. Not only was Mimi a luscious morsel, she was also a rich prize, with her wealthy papa. She should by rights be his.

Mireille disengaged herself and regarded her husband coldly. No, she said, she was far from delighted to see him again. But privately she had to admit that his reappearance was timely. A day or two later and she might have started something with the Englishman, and an affair was complicated and time consuming. On the whole, she thought, she would settle for what she had and make the best of it.

And as for Thornfield, she was under no illusions about his motives. In his own eyes he might be the great seducer, but to her, and to most of the village, he was nothing but a grubby chancer. Being the daughter of a rich *vigneron* had taught Mimi well.

Thornfield left the bar with as much dignity as he could muster.

'I'll show them,' he muttered. 'I'll invite Désirée down from Clermont, *without* the brats. She's a stunner, when she makes the effort. Or I'll ask Clémencie over, she's always saying she wants to see where I live. Or perhaps I'll invite them both! Just think of that oaf's face if I walked in with two beauties on my arm!'

Instead, Fate handed him the perfect revenge.

Gaspard was nearly broke when he got back from Paris. For all his rich pickings during his career as *Le Petit Chat*, he had spent, though discreetly, as freely as he had robbed. He returned with a wardrobe of fine clothes, a small and battered enamel pin with a cat on it, and very little money.

Mimi was not sympathetic.

'No, I'm not going to lend you any money,' she said. 'If you want *fric* you'll have to work for it. Or why don't you take some of your fancy clothes to the *friperie* in St Remy?' she said. 'I'm sure you'll get a good price for Paris fashions, even if they are a little gaudy. After all, where are you going to wear them in Morbignan?'

Gaspard slammed out of the room indignantly, but his wife's words resonated. Why not sell some of the handsome suits and trendy jeans? They would bring in enough to tide him over until he found another source of income. He went to his wardrobe and pulled out the dove grey suit and its matching cap, the first things he had bought in Paris. No, he couldn't bear to part with them.

Next to the suit hung the midnight blue dinner jacket he had worn at the *Bal du Réveillon*. That should bring in a pretty penny: he would take it to the *Frip'* on Saturday. Running his hands over the smooth velvet, he noticed something in the right-hand pocket. It was the white gold and sapphire necklace he had liberated from Sylvie's neck during the waltz. *Merde!* He had forgotten all about it.

Paris was awash with small jewellers in shady corners who didn't enquire too closely into the provenance of any jewel a customer wished to sell. The same could not be said for Morbignan, and even St Rémy was too close for comfort. He would have to go to Clermont l'Hérault and find an accommodating *bijouterie*.

While Gaspard was making elaborate excuses to justify a trip to Clermont, Robin Thornfield was also headed to the big town to see one of his *petites amies*. Clermont l'Hérault is not a big town, but big enough to make a meeting between the two men unlikely. Fate had other ideas.

Jadis. The name over the door said it all: Times Past. The antique and jewellery shop was small and dingy, tucked away in the corner of a small square. Its owner, rejoicing in the serendipitous name of Herr Doktor Goldschmidt, was bent and wizened but his eyes were sharp.

'Here comes a likely one,' he muttered to himself the moment Gaspard entered the shop.

Gaspard produced the necklace.

'It's my aunt's,' he explained. 'She's an old lady in straitened circumstances and she has asked me to sell it for her.'

Goldschmidt took the jewel to the window to examine it more closely; as Fate would have it, a young woman was just about to enter the shop. Seeing the jeweller and what he held in his hands, she gave a little scream and wrenched open the door.

Sylvie Lacoste was in Clermont on an errand: to buy her mother a birthday present. She'd noticed *Jadis* several times while in the town; it looked modest enough to stock something pretty which was within her budget. But now...

'That's my necklace!' she exclaimed. 'It was stolen from me in Paris last New Year's Eve. How do you come to have it?'

'Mademoiselle, you are mistaken,' said Petit at his most suave. 'This trinket belongs to my aunt, who has asked me to sell it for her. There must be many similar baubles like this one but this, I assure you, is not yours.'

Sylvie was insistent. 'No, it's mine. It was a present from *my* aunt, the Marquise de Saint-Esprit. And the man who stole it from me...' she broke off and looked closely at Gaspard.

'Call the police,' she demanded. 'Call the police in Paris and ask for that kind Monsieur Durand. He'll remember me and what happened.'

'One moment.' Goldschmidt disappeared into a back room and returned with a pile of old newspapers. 'I keep these for wrapping parcels,' he explained, 'and I'm sure I saw... yes, yes! Here it is.'

He produced a copy of *Le Parisien* dated January and opened it. Two pages were devoted to the daring robbery at the Hotel George V on New Year's Eve, and the coverage included photographs of the stolen jewels.

'It certainly looks like yours, Mademoiselle,' he said. 'Perhaps we had better call the police after all.'

'You fool!' Petit snarled. 'Your bleary old eyes couldn't tell a sapphire from a hen's egg. That *bijou* is mine, I tell you, and I am not going to stay here and be insulted by the likes of you and this hysterical girl.'

He grabbed the necklace and walked swiftly towards the door. His exit was blocked by a stout man with white hair. A man Petit recognised.

Robin Thornfield was also in Clermont in search of jewellery. He needed something gaudy enough to pacify his girlfriend Désirée but cheap enough to be affordable. He was just debating whether to go into the *bijouterie* when the raised voices inside caught his attention. He decided to investigate.

Entering the shop, he almost cannoned into his hated rival.

'You!' spat both men simultaneously.

Sylvie was weeping quietly into a small white handkerchief. Robin rushed to comfort her.

'Now, what's all this about?' he wanted to know.

Three voices rose in a tangle of explanations, protestations and exclamations. Thornfield listened for a moment, then quietly took the copy of *Le Parisien* from the jeweller's hands. A short perusal told him all he wanted to know.

'So,' he said, '*Le Petit Chat* is it?' Well, that would make a nice story to tell in *l'Estaminet*. What do you think your precious wife and her miser of a father would say if I told them they had a thief in the family? You'd be out on your ear before you could say *Le Petit Chat*.

'I think I'll take care of that,' he continued, and removed the necklace from Petit's hand; with a flourish, he bowed and presented it to Sylvie.

'Yours, I believe, Mademoiselle,' he murmured.

'And as for you,' he turned to Gaspard. 'I'd mind my manners if I were you. You don't want the story getting out, do you? And I think I'll keep this copy of *Le Parisien*, just as insurance.

Sylvie was beside herself. 'Oh, Monsieur, thank you so much. How can I express my gratitude?'

'Well,' he looked into her pretty, tear-stained face, 'You could start by letting me buy you a drink.'

Triumph was within his grasp. What would Mimi's face be like when he walked into the bar with this delicious titbit? He licked his lips at the thought.

Chapter 15

LE PETIT CHAT EST MORT

Morbignan La Crèbe, Saturday

'So that's how I met him,' Sylvie sighed. 'Isn't it strange? You say the policeman met his wife through *Le Petit Chat*, and that's how I met my husband too. Gaspard's got a lot to answer for. Although,' she paused, looking over at Durand, who had his arm round Lili's waist and was laughing at some story Thierry was telling, 'it seems to have worked out better for him than it did for me.

'Robin was quite handsome back then, believe it or not. Do you know, he's had that white hair since he was sixteen. Apparently his mother did too, it runs in the family. Ours was what they call a whirlwind courtship; he swept me off my feet and we were married within three months. Of course, what I didn't realise until too late was that he believed I was very rich. Yes, my aunt is a *Marquise*, but she hasn't got any money to speak of, though of course she pretends to be a *grande dame*. The diamonds were in the *mont-de-piété*, the pawn shop, more often than not.

'Anyway, we got married, and it wasn't long before I found out about all the other women in his life. One of them actually believed he was married to *her*!'

'And yet you've stayed with him all these years?' Betty raised an eyebrow. 'You are either a saint or a very foolish woman.'

'You could say the same for Mireille Petit,' Sylvie retorted. 'Seeing her with Gaspard around the village I've often wondered why she stuck with him. I wonder if she ever found out about *Le Petit Chat*. As for me, I made the best of it, as women do. I have a reasonable home, two lovely children and lots of friends. I go my way and I let Robin go his, though he's finding it harder to be the great seducer these days, now he's getting fat.'

'So what has changed?' Betty said. 'You said he was soon to be your ex. Is that by your choice?'

James Carcenet kicked his mother-in-law in the shin. Sometimes Betty could be too forthright – some might say nosy.

Sylvie sighed.

'You could say Gaspard Petit has something to do with that too. He and Robin have always had history. Robin had a fling with Mimi, Gaspard's wife, when they were much younger, but recently he's been sniffing around her again. I could put up with that, after all I've had enough practice. But now there's this money thing.'

Betty opened her mouth, but James shot her a warning look ad she closed it again. To her gratification, Sylvie continued.

'Robin's awful with money. He's never been in regular employment; he gets odd jobs here and there, but he never keeps them very long. To tell the truth, I've always wondered if he isn't a bit light-fingered. And lately he's started borrowing from everyone who will lend to him, and of course he never pays back.

'Mimi was foolish enough to lend him a thousand euros a while ago. When Gaspard found out he was furious, and he and Robin had an almighty row last week. Robin came home muttering all kinds of threats about what he'd do to him — heaven knows why, because it's he who is in the wrong. Anyway, it will never come to anything, just six-year-olds fighting in the playground, if you ask me.

'But it's started to get really embarrassing. Practically everyone we know is owed money by Robin, and suddenly I realised I'd just had enough. I wish.... What on earth is going on?'

A babble of shrieks and hysterical voices was coming from the terrace. Céleste rushed to open the door, and as everyone crowded round to see what was amiss, two incoherent teenagers burst into the room.

'He's dead, he's dead!' sobbed the girl, shivering in the boy's protective arm.

Lili came forward and took the girl's hands. '*Calme-toi, ma petite,* calm yourself. Who is dead?' she said gently.

The boy made an effort to take charge of the situation. 'Down there,' he said, gesturing behind himself. 'On the steps, *les escaliers*, a dead man.'

Agog and appalled the partygoers trooped down the winding stone staircase that ran from just underneath Thierry's terrace and disappeared round the church.

At the bottom lay Gaspard Petit, his neck bent at an impossible angle. His open eyes stared up into the unseeing sky.

Chapter 16

PATTERSON PUTS TWO AND TWO TOGETHER

Morbignan La Crèbe, three weeks later

Word had gone out. An Announcement was to be made. A dozen or so of the more savvy villagers, those with their ears closest to the ground, had drifted casually in the direction of *l'Estaminet* at this most awkward hour of the evening: too late for even the most determined lingerers over lunch, too early for the six o'clock *apéro*.

'Papa' Pardieu was in his element. The fussy little mayor smoothed his moustache for the third time and looked round at the expectant faces around him.

'*Alors...*' he began. Twelve mouths opened in a gape of anticipation.

'We now have the results of the coroner's enquiry into the untimely death of our fellow *Morbignanais*, Gaspard Petit. The findings are as follows.'

He paused, relishing their attention.

'The findings are that there was nothing untoward in this death; it was, in fact, a tragic accident, no doubt brought on by an excessive consumption of Chateau Rouge-Gorge *rosé*. Monsieur Petit, as we all know, was exceedingly fond of that particular beverage.'

Twelve faces fell. This wasn't the juicy piece of tittle tattle they had been hoping for.

Pardieu went on.

'There was one detail which might have accounted for our friend's tragic demise. On Monsieur Petit's right leg, just above the ankle, was a curious crescent-shaped bruise. One might surmise that the deceased caught his foot on a protruding root, and this caused his fall. However, no such root was seen to be in the vicinity. That being the case, the coroner had no choice but to return a verdict of accidental death by cause unknown.'

Having had his moment, the mayor rose, gave a stiff little bow to the assembled villagers and departed. His secretary Joséphine would be waiting at the *mairie* with his *tisane* and two *madeleines*.

The patrons of *L'Estaminet* broke into a babble of voices as groups formed and excited discussions began.

'In a way, it's the end of an era,' said Richard Patterson, cradling a *demi* and munching on an olive. 'We've all had our issues with Petit — you more than most,' he chuckled, turning to his friend Durand, 'but you have to admit he was one of the village characters.'

'Maybe so,' said James Carcenet, 'but you didn't have to live next to him. He was on the whole quite an unpleasant neighbour. He took against us for some reason, and when he was drunk he used to shout and swear at us in the street. He even cut our phone wires once, and he reported us to the *préfecture* because he said we had cut a window in our end wall without official permission.

'A man arrived from Clermont to investigate and he was most displeased when we showed him the paperwork, signed by our very own mayor! I think he was going to have a strong word with Petit.

'To be honest,' said Betty, 'if someone did do him in, they did us a favour. *Ow!*' James had kicked her sharply in the shins.

Bernard Durand sucked thoughtfully on his pipe. 'I know it's delicious to speculate, but honestly I doubt if it was murder. The brute was drunk most of the time, and it's not surprising if he took a tumble. Ah, here's Lili. She said she might be joining us.'

As the singer made her way towards them, Durand leaned across and, with an expert twist of his wrist, used the curved handle of his walking stick to hook a chair for her from a nearby table.

Richard Patterson stifled a gasp. Watching the manoeuvre, he had a sudden flash of insight. Pardieu's words came back to him: 'A curious crescent-shaped bruise, just above Petit's right ankle.'

He looked at his friend with a wild surmise.

the end

AFTERWORD

From the collected works of Richard Patterson

WHO KILLED THE LITTLE CAT?

Who killed The Little Cat?
'I,' said the wife, 'with my little knife, I killed The Little Cat.'
'I,' said the rival, 'I took up my rifle, and I killed The Little Cat.'
'I,' said the *notaire*, 'with poison to spare, I killed The Little Cat.'
'I,' said the neighbour, 'I borrowed a sabre, and I killed The Little Cat.'
'I,' said the belle, 'I'm happy to tell: I killed The Little Cat.'
'I,' said the poet, 'did you but know it, I killed The Little Cat.'
'I,' said the *flic*, 'for his almighty cheek, I killed The Little Cat.'
'We,' said the steps, 'as downward he crept, we killed The Little Cat.'
'We,' said the stones, 'we broke all his bones, we killed The Little Cat.'

Was it mistress or rival, or the wife he betrayed?
Was it mayor or copper who wielded a blade?
Was it poison or gun shot or was it a fall?
Did one person do it, or perchance was it all?
Who killed The Little Cat?

ABOUT THE AUTHOR

Patricia Feinberg Stoner has been a journalist, advertising copy writer and publicist.

A Londoner to her fingertips, she nevertheless spent four years with her husband and a small brown and white spaniel in Morbignan la Crèbe, a tiny village in the Languedoc. While there, she wrote a series of humorous sketches for a magazine which, in due time, would become her first book, *At Home in the Pays d'Oc*. It chronicles their adventures and misadventures in the region, in a more-or-less factual account of the time they spent there.

At Home in the Pays d'Oc won a Five Star Award from One Stop Fiction and a Reader's Award from Chill with a Book

Tales from the Pays d'Oc is a collection of short stories which revisits Morbignan and the nearby market town of St Rémy les Cévennes. In this new edition, *Murder and Other Tales from the Languedoc*, a brand-new story introduces Gaspard Petit, the most hated man in the village, who is about to meet an untimely end.

Patricia and her husband now live by the sea on the south coast of England. She is the author of three books of comic verse: *Paw Prints in the Butter*, sold in aid of a local animal rescue charity, *Pelicans Can't Read* and *The Little Book of Rude Limericks*.

Patricia welcomes visitors to her Facebook page, Paw Prints in the Butter, and to her blog www.paw-prints-in-the-butter-com.

You may also occasionally find her on Twitter @perdisma.

AT HOME IN THE PAYS D'OC

An English couple excitedly unpack their belongings in their new holiday home. They are at the start of what will be a 30-year adventure; at the end of it their lives will be changed beyond recognition. Now all they have left to do is manhandle an extremely heavy sideboard up an unforgiving flight of stone steps.

'Why don't we roll it up?' she suggests.

He looks at her pityingly, then his eyes widen…

Londoners to the core, they gradually find themselves seduced by the charms and idiosyncrasies of the little village. Over the years they will come to love its steep cobbled streets, its medieval walls, the baker who loves dogs and the *épicière* who opens when she feels like it. They will meet the Velcro bird, the stark-naked builder, the neighbour who cuts the phone lines.

And when a small brown and white dog walks into their lives, they are quite ready to make their home in the Pays d'Oc.

PELICANS CAN'T READ

If you've ever pondered the true identity of Puss in Boots...

wondered why grey geese fly south...

or wanted to know what Santa thinks about Christmas,

 here is where you'll find the answers.

Pelicans Can't Read is a collection of comic verse and limericks on these and other diverse subjects, such as the vagaries of the English language or how to tell dragons apart.